William Melvin Kelley

DIS//INTEGRATION

William Melvin Kelley was born in New York City in 1937 and attended the Fieldston School and Harvard. The author of four novels and a short story collection, he was a writer in residence at the State University of New York at Geneseo and taught at The New School and Sarah Lawrence College. He was awarded the Anisfield-Wolf Book Award for lifetime achievement and the Dana Reed Prize for creative writing. He died in 2017.

BY WILLIAM MELVIN KELLEY

A Different Drummer

A Drop of Patience

dem

Dunfords Travels Everywheres

Dancers on the Shore (short stories)

DIS//INTEGRATION

DIS//INTEGRATION

2 Novelas & 3 Stories & a Little Play

William Melvin Kelley

riverrun

First published in the United States in 2024 by Penguin Random House LLC
This paperback edition first published in Great Britain in 2024 by

riverrun

An imprint of
Quercus Editions Limited
Carmelite House
50 Victoria Embankment
London EC4Y 0DZ

An Hachette UK company

The authorised representative in the EEA is Hachette Ireland,
8 Castlecourt Centre, Castleknock Road, Castleknock,
Dublin 15, D15 YF6A, Ireland

A portion of this work was originally published
in *Dunfords Travels Everywheres* (Doubleday, 1970).

A CIP catalogue record for this book is available
from the British Library

PB ISBN 978 1 52943 897 0
EBOOK ISBN 978 152943 898 7

1

Printed and bound in Great Britain by Clays Ltd, Elcograf S.p.A.

MIX
Paper | Supporting responsible forestry
FSC® C104740
www.fsc.org

Papers used by Quercus are from well-managed forests and other responsible sources.

For Aiki the Brave:

Fierce-browed, I coolly defy a thousand pointing fingers.
Head-bowed, like a willing ox I serve the children.

—Lu Xun

Only that day dawns to which we are awake. There is more day to dawn. The sun is but a morning star.

—Henry David Thoreau

Hold to the now, the here, through which all future plunges to the past.

—James Joyce

DIS//INTEGRATION

JUNE

1952

time I surprise people who don't know me very well by calling myself a feminassist. They wonder how an old bachelor literary historian can espouse such radical views as equal pay for equal work, and even equal pay for comparable work, though occasionally I have trouble with the comparable part. But I more surprise them by assuring them that my feminassistism runs deeper than even money. I genuinely believe that in any way men care to define it, women bear half the responsibility for everything that humankind has destroyed or accomplished.

I didn't always feel that way. I had a good traditional education. So naturally I started out believing in the superiority of men and never thought to look behind any of the renowned men of history to see if any female lurked there, exerting strong influence. Now I know better. Whether or not we know their names, and even though they themselves don't always know it, women stand there behind or beside men, contributing equally to humankind's development.

I owe credit for sowing the first seeds of my feminassistism to my paternal grandmother, Nanny Eva Dunford, whom

I met for the first time at seventeen years of age in 1952. We never had any hard evidence establishing her date of birth. She maintained that missionaries had brought her from Africa in 1866 at the age of four. But we always suspected that an 1872 birth date seemed more likely. Still, she could have come from Africa. She seemed to have no European ancestry: both my father (years ago) and myself (more recently) have searched unsuccessfully for a record of her parents..And she did give us the name of the missionaries, a couple named Willson (with two l's). I had an exchange of letters with the Willson family, but they didn't give much help. All to say that Nanny Eva knew her Bible as well as any scholar. She knew it cold and hot, Pentateuch and Revelation. Quote a phrase from the Bible and she could cite chapter and verse. If it had multiple citations, she would know that too. "Isaiah quotin David, son," she would say, amazing me.

Nanny Eva Dunford lived with my uncle GL and his wife Rose in a near mansion high up on a hill in New Marsails. Segregation and all! With little education but with an engaging personality, Uncle GL had already made and lost three fortunes. In 1952, he owned a bar, a record store and a taxi service. So they lived well, even though they could not sip from certain drinking fountains. Irony.

A few days after my father and I had arrived from New York, Nanny Eva and I found ourselves out on the verandah overlooking New Marsails and the Gulf beyond. She looked clean and crisp, chocolate brown and shiny skinned with kinky white hair like a cloud framing her fierce-eyed face. I felt moved to take some photos of her with my little Argoflex box camera. I excused myself and went inside to get it, then returned to the verandah.

"Now, son, Nanny don'want no pictures! Just take that box camera right back inside!"

I told her she looked extremely photogenic and begged her to let me take some pictures, thinking that I might not have too many more chances. She looked strong, but had lived at least eighty years.

"Don'want no pictures took I tell you." She pursed her lips, squinted. "Don'need none."

But I needed them, I insisted. Her two other grandchildren, my brother Peter and my sister Connie, had only one faded snapshot of her, taken in the 1930s. We needed something more recent.

"Might break yo camera," she warned. "Busted every camera ever took a picture o me. Ugly like mud. No Lena Vaughn. So 'less you don'plan on takin pictures afta this . . ." She held the *s*, hissing.

I promised her I'd only take a few, though I wanted to take a whole roll of twelve. I asked her to sit up straight and smooth her skirt over her lap.

She shot me a fiery glance. "Makin' me look like a glamour girl? Easy to see you don'have no respect for no women cept as glamour girls."

I protested, asking her if I'd disrespected her since meeting her.

"Not me, you better not, but our kind, womankind. I done hear what you said last night afta supper. Didn'think Rose n me could hear, but we could hear you bold." Nanny Eva sucked her tongue. "Bout them five Jewish men startin everythin."

It hit me. After supper the night before, while the women cleared the table and washed the dishes, pretty-faced Aunt Rose bustling, Nanny Eva doing what she could at a slower pace, the men, Uncle GL and my father and I sitting at the dining room table, had conducted wide-ranging intrafamilial and intergenerational discussions, during the course of which the subject of the Jews came up. Uncle GL stood opposed. I doubt if he'd even met a Jew in his largely segregated life, but he blamed the Jews for the recent World War II. My father objected strenuously. He'd lived in New York City for a quarter century, coming to the conclusion that the Jews meant no harm, and occasionally helped Africamerica. Seventeen years old and snotty-nosed, I ventured an opinion expressed in the hallways of my private school, by students if not faculty, that all Western thought had evolved out of the philosophies of five Jewish men: Moses-Jesus-Marx-Freud-and-Einstein. Now Nanny Eva had taken offense.

"Five Jewish men startin everythin! Zifwomen didn'have no say in the world. What bout blessed Jesus Mama Mary? What the Catholics do widout her? Bet you never wonder why Creator God want to bring in Jesus by Mary, stead o just make him wid mud like he done Adam. Cos it done need a woman. N done forget bout sis Jochebed."

I had followed her until the last. Lost a moment, my nervous index finger had squeezed off a shot, the first of the roll, which developed slightly blurred, her eyes wide open and eyebrows raised.

"Moses Mama. Saved the world n didn'get no credit fo it. Know why?" Some ideas take time to get through to me. Others come like lightning. Jokerbed (later I learned the correct spelling), mother of Moses, saved the world? Inwardly I scoffed as only a private school brat can scoff.

"Cos men write the story when it all said n done did. So they make it look like men save the day. Women steppin in when the goin get so bad only a woman can save it. Nobody thinkin bout writin it down when Hard Times holdin court. Everybody too busy scramblin. N women the best scramblers, eggs n otherwise. Cos women the first n best experimenters. Now put that box camera away n tell Nanny Eva what you want fo yo dinner!"

I tried to divert her, pointing out that I'd thought she wanted to tell me about Jochebed, the mother of Moses, unless perhaps Nanny Eva really had nothing worthwhile to say about this little-known woman.

Well, I shouldn't have said that. The heat coming out of her eyes seemed to jelly the air between us. "Nothin worth sayin? Bout Moses Mama? Why son, what the most hard times you ever know?" While I thought of an answer, I took a second shot, the old lady glaring at me, really the top of my head as I bent looking into the viewfinder.

"Ever been a slave? Well, I never did actually be one, but did know plenty was as a girl n they told me all bout it. First off they buyin n sellin you like bulls and cows. Workin a place twenty years n have some roots, a good man n some chilren, then the owner dyin on you n the greedy relations come swoopin down sayin, I want the strong one n I want the cook n I will take that little cutie over there. Now who you think done have the hardest time in slavery? Why the women, son. A man, cept fo the few has some backbone, just thinkin bout keepin self alive. A woman thinkin bout keeping chilren n self alive. Double duty n please her owner too!

"Folks talk bout the driver lash, but Nanny Eva consider the pain to the soul. Livin in the tornado n keepin yo fear n heat inside. Get beat but forbid to cry. Some folks raise they chilren that way. Bad business! Least when I done wail my chilren I let them wail." She fell silent, studying a spot on the verandah floor, her hands folded. I snapped photo no. three, an image I've treasured ever since.

The click broke her reverie. "Better pack that thing away." But a droll smile disrupted her stern face. "Got me good, didn'you?"

I wound forward to no. four, saying probably condescendingly that I found her analysis of slavery illuminating. Most commentators emphasized the abstract concept of freedom and the physical pain. But they would've loved slavery as a soul-distorting experience in ethics class at the Shaddy Bend School.

"I done miss some o that comin over in 1866 wid the Reverend Willson, but I done catch hell in the Reconstruction. Not to say the Willsons didn'beat me regular, but like parents. Least they done say so n I believe them cos they give me Creator God, n the Bible n teach me to read."

Her face went quiet and peaceful, her gaze tender under still black eyebrows, looking straight at me. I took photo no. four and wound forward to no. five.

"Sis Jochebed had Creator God too. Cos remember she be raise up in the tribe o Levi, tribe all the priests come from. Back befo Moses invent Hebrew n write anythin down, when the Hebrew chilren talkin they religion. Didn'have no time to read n write. Just be workin is all, makin n haulin brick fo the pyramids. Cos the Hebrew chilren be brought real low from Joseph time. Now Pharoah purely want to kill they boy babies. Even we didn'have it that bad in slavery times, when a baby boy o good stock worth much as sixty dollars. Killin boy babies be like burnin money. So you see how desperate be those times fo the Hebrew chilren. Worth not a thing!

"Now here be Jochebed wid two chilren n a new one comin. Already had a boy, Aaron, workin at the pyramids. The girl Miriam safe fo now cos she hasn'reach breedin age yet. Now Jochebed pregnant n tryin not to look it, hidin her belly under dresses n skirts. Didn'want the Egyptian baby police to stop her on the street n give her a belly check. If they find she carryin they watch her n send somebody round to see if it come out a boy n kill it."

Her face looked grim as she leaned forward, whispering, conspiring with Jochebed and me to see the baby born and spared. I wanted to take photo no. five but didn't want the thunder of the shutter to break her spell. "She give birth quiet like a cat, get the baby to cry, then get it to stop. Didn'want nobody to hear. She done have a midwife she could trust to keep her secret, probably old Auntie Shiphrah know her from a girl. Wouldn'betray her no matta how much they pay. Look in they faces n flat-out lie. No sir, I never hear bout no boy baby born down our lane. Anyway the Hebrew women has they babies n hide them befo we even get there."

Photo no. five captured the look of a righteous woman lying through her teeth, back straight, lips tight, above reproach.

"Then she had to hide him fo three months. Had a little crawl space she stuff him into whenever anybody she couldn'trust come to visit. Dress him like a girl when she have to take him out. Told his sister Miriam to call him Dinah afta Jacob daughter whenever anybody spicious come snoopin.

"When he reach three months old n start to gettin rambunctious, she had one of them dreams biblical folks has when Creator God want to tell them somethin.

"She dream she walkin down to the river Nile wid a load o clo'es fo washin when she come up on two women wid they feet dangling in the water. One she done know right away as Sarah, wife o Abraham. Other one she didn'know at first. Well findin herself in the company o holy women, Jochebed fall on her knees n worship. But pretty quick they pull her up n make her sit down beside them, all three wid they feet in the water. Told her to cool her feet cos her line would do a heap o walkin. Then they tells her to build a little boat. Round this time Jochebed realize she dreamin, knowin how you know sometime, n she say to herself, That sound ridicalous! Must be dreamin. O course you dreamin, Sarah say, how else you ever get to meet me? But you still needin a little boat. Real fancy, painted colorful wid interestin designs all over it, the other holy woman say. Take a little time wid it but you hasn'got much time. Jochebed couldn'make no sense o it. Why she needin a fancy little boat?"

Nanny Eva hardly noticed me squeezing off photo no. six, giving me an exasperated fleeting smile.

"Build it to see what'll happen, say the other holy woman, who Jochebed reco'nize as Mama Eve, wife o Adam. Got to take a chance like Noah wife, specially when Hard Times holdin court. Sometimes even when you livin in Paradise. So build the boat n make it fancy. But then what? Jochebed aksin but wakin up befo Mama Sarah even give a answer.

"So she commence to buildin a little boat, like a big covered basket, weavin it from grasses. Now the Bible say she done smear it wid slime, which could be mud or tar, to make it watertight. Then she paint it, red-yellow-blue-purple, rainbow colors, n stud it wid pretty stones, so a body could see it glitterin n twinklin a long way off."

Her face turned thoughtful, a woman at her crafts, in the concentration of creation, deciding just where to put a stone or bit of glass; I squeezed off no. seven.

"But she still didn'know why she possess a fancy little boat n the baby police be getting mo spicious every day.

"Now Miriam big sister to Moses one o them wanderin chilren. No fence or chain keep them from wanderin. Had two such girls as that myself. Then they get marry n settle right down, never leave the house. Anyway in her wanderin, Miriam done go down to the river Nile, Main Street to Egypt in those times, to watch the fishermen mendin they nets n sellin they fish n all the other activities on the riverside. Since no fence could keep her from wanderin where her heart want to wander, she have adventure through reeds to a beautiful cove where Pharoah daughter had a little swimmin pool builded right into the riverbank n would swim butt nekid wid a gang o her women.

"Miriam done get home late that evenin. Jochebed meetin her at the door wid a strap in her hand, aksin her where she been. Pretty quick Miriam tellin her mama all bout Pharoah daughter swimmin butt nekid in the river Nile n Jochebed forget whippin on her, cos soon as she done hear bout Pharoah daughter, a whole plan come to her. Cos the thing bout rich folks you can never get to see them less you work fo them. So she thankin the holy women o her dreams cos they done look into the future n give Jochebed a glimpse too."

Nanny Eva's face relaxed into the contentment of a woman who feels herself at one with universal forces. She hardly noticed or cared that I took photo no. eight.

"So now Moses Mama have a plan n the next day she start to make it real. She put her baby boy in his best little outfit, combin his hair n all. Then she take him n put him into the fancy little boat the holy women done have her build, tied him into it case it tip over. Then she took Miriam n tie a long leather tether to her wrist n tie the other end to the little boat. Miriam would steer it down the river Nile n into the cove where Pharoah daughter swimmin butt nekid.

"She kiss them both n bless them n send them down the river Nile, Miriam on the shore holdin the leather tether n the baby Moses in his fancy little boat. From the riverbank, Miriam coaxin the little boat into the cove where Pharoah daughter did her swimmin butt nekid. Then Miriam loose the leather tether n hide n watch the little boat drift into Pharoah daughter cove."

She fell silent, staring out at the Gulf. I took no. nine, and it did not disturb her. I leaned forward to see if she had fallen asleep.

"Plan went pretty well afta that. The glittery little boat done catch Pharoah daughter eye n she fetch it to her n see the baby Moses n fell right on in love. Even though she know by his little circumcize peepee that he come from the Hebrews. Must o been a cute healthy little baby boy, considerin what he to become. Dazzled her wid his big smile n bright face, Moses aft'all.

"Round this time in the general hustle n bustle made by the fancy boat n bright little boy, baby Moses get hungry n commence to cry. Miriam pop up n get him to quiet down n smile his big smile, which impress Pharoah daughter. Right then n there, she offer Miriam a job takin care o her new adopted son. Jochebed had done told Miriam what to say next. Say she know a woman who just lost her child to the baby police n she still have milk n maybe she would wet nurse this baby til he old enough to eat solid food. Pharoah daughter like the plan."

Nanny Eva sat up straight and eager, the girl Miriam doing as her mother had instructed; I snapped no. ten.

"So home they all went, the baby Moses n sister Miriam n some palace guards to get them there, back to they very own house. At first, Jochebed pretend like she didn'want Pharoah daughter baby to suck the milk o the baby she lost to the baby police. But afta while, the palace guards talk her into it, tell her Pharoah daughter command it. So she give in. The palace guards left her wid her baby Moses, now Pharoah daughter son, n Miriam along wid a wagonload o food n new clo'es. Right back home where they start out from that mornin. Protected from the baby police!" She leaned back, laughed, and patted her thighs with her hands, which seemed carved from baker's chocolate. I clicked no. eleven. "So if five Jewish men start everythin you got to put a Hebrew woman Jochebed in there wid them, cos she begat Moses n save him a couple times, startin wid gettin him safe n protected inside Pharoah palace. Now what man would make up a plan like that?"

From that moment on, though I did not always know or act it, I surrendered to feminassistism. Since then the concept of female historical equality has never strayed far from my consciousness, though in my personal relationships I've done as many stupid-ass things as any man.

I took no. twelve, the last of the roll, the next day. Nanny Eva and I found ourselves on the verandah again. She had a lot of energy that morning and I ran to get my camera. When I returned, she pointed her finger at me. "She save him another time when he kill that man. Had two such hot-blooded sons as that myself. Shoot men over somethin foolish! But they yo boys n you got to save them. So how you think Moses get away when he kill that man?" She raised her finger beside her twinkling eye; I clicked no. twelve and told her I did not know.

"Cos you didn'listen, son. Moses Mama dress him like a woman!" So from that time . . .

APRIL
1963

time I lived in Reupeo, I saw a little boy (who thought he was a horse) cry, which for him was almost as good as if he'd smiled. I called him Chuvo, which means "horse" in Reupeonese. I didn't know his real name. I called him Chuvo because he did everything a horse does, all on two seven-year-old legs. He walked, trotted, cantered and galloped like a horse. He whinnied and neighed like a horse. And the first time I tried to touch him, like a horse that doesn't want to be touched, he bit me.

I hadn't realized he was serious about his horse impersonation until he did that, and when he did, I cursed him. But he just stood there on the sidewalk in front of the Cafe of One Hand, staring at me, like a horse.

"That's not nice," I told him in Reupeonese. His teeth had marked my hand.

He snorted, not meaning insult, but like a horse. When a boy who thinks he's a horse snorts, I don't take it personally; he snorted.

"Good morning, little boy," I tried again.

He shuffled his feet around, looking my way, but not at me.

I decided to ignore him, returning to my newspaper (*Lua Jornala dol Madjona*) and my little white cup of espresso coffee. But after I'd finished both my cup and the article I'd been reading, and looked up, he was still there, his head inclined loosely on his rigid little neck.

"So you're a horseboy." I stood up and stretched, after sitting in the Cafe most of the morning.

The waiter saw me getting set to go and came over. After he counted my saucers and told me what I owed him, I asked him about the horseboy. "Does he ever stop—"

"Being a horse? Never, my sir. I have worked mornings in this cafe for three years, at least a year before he began to prance up and down on the sidewalk, and never have I seen him be anything but a horse!"

"Do you know his name?"

"No, my sir, I call him Horse."

Chuvo.

At the time, I was involved in a casual relationship with a girl who lived not far from the Cafe around two corners but crossing no streets. I didn't have anything I had to read for my Dupukshamin thesis that afternoon, so I decided to walk around to see if she'd arrived home from her morning classes. I paid the waiter and started off. Chuvo followed me, at a trot. Sometimes he would move out ahead of me, but soon he would wheel, passing me going the other way, then catch up again.

My friend was home, but in a bad mood. I asked her about Chuvo.

"O please, Chig, I haven't any idea. The boy's obviously troubled deeply, or worse. He follows me in the morning."

I smiled.

"But Chig, it's frightening, as I make my bleary-eyed way to the underground, to have a boy who thinks he is a horse, galloping and snorting at my heels."

"I love the way you put things."

"Do you? Why?"

"Because you are so clear, in a Baroque kind of way."

"I find you Romanesque. Do you want a drink before you go?"

"No thanks, but listen. I have an extra reupeo or two. You want to go out to dinner tonight?"

"I've got an engagement tonight, Chig." She put her hand on my arm. "Sorry."

"It's all right."

She walked me to the door, her arm around my waist. "Actually, I'd rather stay in; I'm three books behind myself. And dinner with you would be nice."

"Why go out?"

"Because he needs me more." She stared at me. "Understand?"

I nodded. "I'll come by next week."

"Do." She paused. "On second thought, don't wait that long." She hugged me with lots of body.

Downstairs, I found Chuvo. He cantered with me along the sidewalk back around past the Cafe of One Hand as far as the section of Roman viaduct, which straddles the narrow street. When I stepped down onto the cobblestones, he stopped.

I stopped too. "That your mother forbids the horse to go into the street?" I asked in Reupeonese.

He didn't answer, of course, just turned and galloped away.

Over the next few months, what with mornings in the Cafe and visits to my friend, I saw quite a lot of Chuvo. Only interrupted by the viaduct, the sidewalk ran all the way around the block, passing the Cafe, and my friend's building; but no matter where I set foot on that sidewalk, he would appear, colting in circles.

He never smiled. But how many of us have seen horses smile. Some claim they have, I know. Horse lovers. But I'm not a horse lover. Which doesn't mean that I dislike horses. I don't know them very well. Horses are a luxury in cities, where I have always lived, though I know people who have horses, to ride, in cities.

I don't know horses or whether they smile, I've never seen it, but this was a boy, not a horse, who never smiled. But I could touch him now, pat his head, as I pat a horse's head, respectfully. And he had begun to let me feed him cubes of sugar.

That was the only human thing he did consistently, the way he ate sugar cubes. He would circle in close toward the sugar on my outstretched palm, go through all the motions of eating it horse-fashion, then quick pick it up in his hand, check it for dirt up near his eye, pop it into his mouth; and back to horse.

Once I left the wrapper on the sugar cube. He took it off so fast I never learned where he put it, then back to horse.

I got to like him. As a horse he was a heck of a boy. So when my friend told me she was leaving the city for good, robbing me of sixtysix percent of the reason why I studied at the Cafe in the mornings instead of at one of Smepriroa's many libraries, I knew I wouldn't see Chuvo as much as I had. I guess that's why he sticks in my mind—because the last time I saw him was the last time I saw her.

My friend had told me over dinner that she had been asked to some kind of family reunion in Rome, her friend's family, and because she felt her life settling into a bloody awful rut and wanted some change of scene, she had decided to accept the invitation; from Rome she would go someplace else, but she wouldn't return to Smepriroa.

"That's short notice."

"You won't miss me, love."

"I will because I'm used to you." I liked her because I could say things like that to her.

"Just your old mattress." She turned serious. "I'm sure you understand this isn't a life for me. I shan't be taking courses forever. I think I'd better get on to my real life, don't you see."

"Of course. When are you leaving?"

"Tomorrow morning."

"Wow." That was short notice.

"I think you're moved, Chig."

"I am."

She smiled catlike. "Then you'd better take me home. I still have packing to do. And eventually I must get some sleep."

Outside the restaurant, feeling romantic, I suggested we take a horse and carriage, across the Bridge of Towers and along the river, to her place.

"What a silly idea. You spend too much time in books. Let's!" We walked to the fountain, where the hack drivers park in ambush for the tourists. "And that's true, you know. Things which only happen in books are things you do."

"Like what?"

"Like taking a horse-drawn carriage because your friend is going away. How absurd!"

We woke up a hackey and asked him to drive us. He climbed out of the back, up onto his high seat, and we got in. Despite the cobblestones, the ride wasn't bouncy, which surprised me, but I did think we weren't going very fast. I asked the hackey about it.

He cursed and how for two minutes. "This stupid animal

has been eating at my liver this entire day, my sir. Worthless! I would take him to the glue factory except that I know they'd reject his wormy toes."

"But a horse hasn't toes." My friend was lightheaded, an occasional state.

"He has the split toes of Satan. Of this I assure you, miss."

"I shouldn't talk like that about someone who helps you make a decent living."

The hackey made a sour face and turned back to his driving, snapping his whip across the horse's back. But it didn't make the horse go faster. By the time we entered the Street of the Viaduct, the animal was hardly moving at all.

I was disappointed because I had wanted to see Chuvo with a horse, like an experiment to test the depth of his impersonation. Now the horse I'd hired seemed less of a horse than Chuvo.

I told the hackey to stop in front of the Cafe; we'd walk the rest of the way. I stepped out, looking for Chuvo, then helped my friend to the cobblestones.

Meanwhile, the horse died. I tell it that way because it happened that way. We stepped down, then I heard the traces creak, looked, and the horse had dropped to its knees. Then it fell over to its side. Then it was dead with a sigh.

"Wow."

"Poor thing." My friend looked genuinely sad.

The hackey turned livid. He jumped down off the seat and started to kick the horse in the head. I confess it, I winced.

"Stop that!" my friend shouted at the hackey. "Chig, make him stop."

The hackey was kicking the horse so hard that I was glad the horse was dead and couldn't feel. "Hey, stop!" I shouted in English.

Chuvo galloped up. It was about an hour before dark; restaurants served dinner early in Reupeo. So Chuvo was still down on the sidewalk. He galloped up and stood, pawing, pawing, snorting, watching the hackey kick the dead horse.

Then he charged and started to kick at the hackey with such force that sometimes he lost his balance and fell on his backside, a little boy in short pants fighting a man. Finally my friend went up to them, pulled Chuvo away with the grip of a schoolteacher, then put her other hand softly on the hackey's arm. "Enough, my sir. The animal cannot feel your hate."

"Hate? I'm trying to wake him." He covered his face with his hands. "I want to wake him. Satan, get up. If you please."

My friend came back to me, leading Chuvo. "Suppose we could buy him a hot chocolate, Chig?"

"Sure."

But Chuvo had gone back to horse, twisting away from my friend, racing up the block and around the corner. By the time we reached the corner, already trying to ease the pain of the incident with little jokes, he had disappeared into one of the street's many doorways.

The next time I went back to the Cafe, the waiter told me he'd heard that the boy's mother had sent him to live with an aunt in the provinces, kind of putting Chuvo out to pasture.

I realize I forgot to tell the most interesting part of the story. When he was kicking the hackey, Chuvo was crying. Do horses cry? I've never seen it, though one time . . .

AUGUST
1964

time possessed him—he always carried two watches, one on his wrist and one in his pocket. "If you know the time," he once said, punching my breastbone, "you know how far you reached on the way to Mother Death's cottage in the forest. Getting late. So let's do a couple things before we get there."

One of the things John Hoenir did, he sparred, and since it takes two to spar, he'd challenge somebody to spar, his challenge usually but not always very formal. If one accepted the challenge, then one wanted to spar too, his point exactly.

Hoenir believed that a well-balanced man should develop ways to express his physicality against other men without having to kill. So he loved contact sports, football, boxing, wrestling; he liked to knock up against people. "They don't respond to words anymore; you have to touch them hard!"

The first evening we met, Hoenir tried to get me to spar with him. But obviously I have my weight problem, the tendency of my seat to spread, so Hoenir's proposal that we spar (he looked in good shape, a wiry sandyhaired middleweight) made me unhappily aware of my own body, at the same time as the absurdity of the image of myself sparring with anybody made me laugh.

"You don't get the point, kid." Hoenir's eyes narrowed to slits.

Wanting to take his mind off sparring and believing I recognized his accent, I asked him if he'd grown up in New York City.

"Not New York City, kid, the Bronx. But I cleared out a long time ago to go to college. Then I got married and we traveled all over until two years ago we settled down here in Smepriroa." He shook his head, smiling. "But don't think you can make me forget our fight, kid. I got lots of bad gas to blow off."

But why challenge me to step outside onto the cobblestone street to puff, to sweat, perhaps to receive injury? I hadn't said one word to him, had never seen him before that evening of the Sunday of the Assassination when he marched up to my table in the Cafe of One Hand and challenged me to spar.

"Because the minute I came through the door I could tell you had bad gas to blow off." He tapped his chest. "Me too."

Assuming he believed I had the Assassination on my mind, I commented that whatever we might feel about the news from the States, I doubted our feelings would evaporate into the sticky August air because we used each other's faces for whipping boys.

"When did you try it the last time? Gets off subway loads of bad gas. Anyway I didn't mean the murder. But maybe because of it. Something else happened to you today; you learned a lesson about yourself. Go on, kid, tell me I read you wrong."

Actually he'd read me quite right; I asked him how he knew. "Written all across your mug, kid. In fact you look like you learned a lot today. So don't waste our time; let's just dance around and trade punches until we forget the rest of this crap." He hesitated, then pointed a stiff freckled finger at my forehead. "Come to think of it, I do want to get your opinion about this murder."

The Assassination; but which aspect of it did he want my opinion on? And would he sit down at my table and share my half litre of wine?

"Thanks." He sat across from me and rested on the table between us his speckled notebook a bit larger than his freckled hand. "Pick your aspect, kid."

Then I found it ironical that someone would kill a President of the United States at a baseball game, I told him.

"You consider that ironical?" Hoenir poured himself a full glass of wine. "Just necessary, kid, that choice of place. Knowing he liked the game enough to go at least one time a week, and that no one could get close to him inside of anywhere. But you know what gets me?

"Imagine yourself sitting in your special presidential baseball box, your family around you, enjoying the game, the atmosphere, that green nightlit grass, and the bugs swarming around those grids of light, and the white ball way up there, then curving down into a golden glove made from the best leather in the world.

"Inning's over: everybody running but the pitchers, eighteen guys each with a different place to go. Then the lights flutter, and you lick your ice cream cone, and you wonder, because you do wonder about it: Does the end come now?

"Because, face it, every profession has a type of violent death attached to it. Naturally, Lincoln, Garfield and McKinley cross your mind a couple times a month. You wonder about it; you ponder on it, especially those gray days when you look up from the world on your desk and out the window at the rain dropping on the roses.

"But not usually at the ball game you don't, not on a warm summer night, writing an F-8 in the diamond on your scorecard—until the lights flicker, then go out: Does the end come now?

"But the lights come back on, a tub of brightness surrounded by the city, and you shiver, suddenly cold, hoping the wife and the bodyguard didn't see you, saying to yourself: not now.

"Only then do you see the four groundskeepers (they look like) who stare at you, the brooms they hoist turning into shotguns: now, mother F! *Blam!!!!*" Up jumped our glasses and the half litre of wine, nearly empty, to the slam of Hoenir's hand. "The end comes now!"

I took a deep breath, told him I still didn't understand which aspect of the Assassination most interested him.

"Can't you see the point, kid? In the last instant of his life, when he saw the guns, he knew he wouldn't go to Heaven. His enemies hated him that much."

I must have looked puzzled.

Hoenir leaned toward me, his graybrown eyes steady on mine. "You can only go to Heaven if you die fighting. An ambush don't count." He drained then refilled his glass with the last of the wine, drained his glass again, head back, a wave of sandyhair flat to his forehead, then stood up. "Come on, kid."

I hadn't forgotten that I didn't want to spar, I told him.

"I withdraw my challenge." He picked up his speckled notebook, then came around the table and grabbed my elbow with plierslike fingers. "I got more than one way to blow off bad gas. Hey, tell me your name."

I introduced myself, getting up.

He let go my elbow, extended his right hand. "Hoenir, Johannes Bernhardi, born in the Bronx the seventeenth of June 1935."

"Wow," I said. "The same day as me." Myself in Manhattan at nine; Hoenir in Fordham Hospital at four. I shook his hand; he crushed mine.

"Sure, Charlie, I knew we had something between us soon as I came through the door and saw you sitting alone getting drunk."

I started to protest my innocence, but Hoenir cut me off.

"Hey, kid, every man has the right to get drunk from time to time. Better a headache than a heartache."

I laughed somewhat uneasily and together we left the Cafe of One Hand, climbing the slope to Beulward dol Touras, Smepriroa's main street, strangely still at this evening's hour, though small knots of men grouped in the shadows whispered harshly over the afternoon's epoch-shattering event.

"Let's walk around, kid, and get the feel of the town." Hoenir's invitation came wrapped in a backhand punch to my upper arm. "Another good way to blow off bad gas. Some afternoons I walk off twenty miles of bad gas: from my place up to the Towers, then back around the Truvo side of the promontory Smepriroa's sitting on, then over the ridge Tower Boulevard runs along, and down the hill to where the Seurno bellies out; I'll sit outside a bar on the riverbank, looking across at the slums where a couple very good painters live because of the big cheap rooms.

"After I finish my drink, I'll walk along the left bank of the Seurno as it rushes to meet the Truvo, past the base of the Towers, along the river's rocky shore past the Castle of Ruins, to the arrow tip of the city, where Seurno and Truvo join to become the broad Truvoseurno on her way to the sea; then down the Truvo's right bank again, around the curve to the bridge to the island and up the hill to my courtyard; then'll do it again, just walking, looking, thinking. Some days I walk my feet numb. But you can sure blow off bad gas walking when you can't find someone to fight."

In any case, all that geography can't mean much to you since you've never visited Smepriroa. Suffice to say that John Hoenir did a lot of walking as well as a lot of sparring, but even so, found the time to write . . .

SEPTEMBER 1964

time as any to correct an imbalance in the picture one might have gained concerning the life John Hoenir led in Smepriroa. Certainly he spent several hours each afternoon in the street, walking, knocking up against people, sparring, but every morning he gave to his writing.

I guess most of the time he wrote at home: two large neat rooms with whitewashed walls and red tile floors, a living-room window that gulped sun from ten til two, a tiny terrace out from the bedroom where Hoenir worked; and overlooking romantic Reupeon ruins.

Then too at the time he had a wife: "Hey, she'll really like you, kid. Class impresses her more than it does me," Hoenir said of her as we climbed the steps to the door of their apartment, nine hours after our meeting at the Cafe of One Hand.

Hoenir'd taken me to a dozen places, all of them packed with people listening to radios for the news from the States. I hadn't known that many students, secretaries, painters and poets, designers, dancers, actresses and accountants from places like Seattle, Peoria, Des Moines, and Albuquerque lived in Smepriroa. But Hoenir seemed to know every one of them.

After we'd done all the walking and visiting, Hoenir insisted I accompany him to meet his wife, at six a.m. Monday morning.

But wouldn't we wake her? I asked him.

"Not a chance, kid. Freddi can't sleep unless I'm in bed too." He pressed his doorbell with his thumb.

His wife opened the door; fully dressed in a black Glen plaid skirt and a brown turtleneck sweater. "Good morning, John. You left your key behind." She extended the key, the old long type.

Hoenir took it. "Why do I need a key when you stay home all the time?"

She stared at him from under the tawny bangs that hid her brows. "One day you might find me gone out."

"Then I'll wait for you." Hoenir smiled, shrugged. "Hey, did you hear some guys murdered the President?"

"Whose President?" She scowled at him. "Surely not ours. How horrible everything's become." She turned toward me, offering her hand. "Excuse my husband's poor manners. I'm Freddi."

I shook her hand, told her my name, let go her smooth strong cold hand.

"How about that! Ambushed him at a ball game with shotguns. Wonder what Denn Gainnacht would say if he still lived." Hoenir stepped into the apartment, leaving his wife and me in the hallway, then called back: "Hey, Freddi, can you make some food? I forgot to eat."

I told his wife I thought I should go home.

She took my wrist. "But you must have some scrambled eggs before you do. John! Come tell Chig Dunford he can't go until he's had something. If only some coffee."

Hoenir did not respond; she pulled me gently into their apartment.

"Do you like Smepriroa?" She seated me in a chair at a round table in the livingroom. Before I had time to express my feelings on that strangest of European capital cities, I heard coming from the bedroom the uneven punches of small iron fists against paper: Hoenir at his Corona typewriter.

After a moment, Freddi Hoenir went to speak to him and returned to say: "John wants us to go on and eat without him. He's started a novel."

I stood up, said I needed sleep now more than food, and headed for the door.

"Chig Dunford don't be silly, John writes only one page each day, which usually takes him somewhat less than two hours. By the time you and I talk a bit, then I fix something to eat, and serve it, John will have finished for the day, and we can all do something wonderful together."

I told her I really thought it best that I go, so Hoenir could work.

"John will work come what may." She smiled, bit her lower lip, then sighed. "But my father taught me never to try to change a man's mind."

It seemed a good lesson for a father to teach his daughter, I commented.

"How nice of you to say so, Chig Dunford." She opened the door for me.

"Did John invite you to our party? I'm sure he forgot. Next month we'll have been married seven years and we're giving a big party." She told me a date in September, instructed me to arrive any time after four in the afternoon. "Please do come, Chig Dunford."

I promised her I would, and did, arriving fashionably late at four thirty to find the Hoenirs' two rooms jammed; one hundred people in each room, and a hundred more making a second livingroom of the hallway outside their door.

The Hoenirs gave a good party, with a wine and liquor table in each room, lots of salty snacks, caviar, crackers, five kinds of cheese and a Brazilian they'd paid to play bossa nova and Bach on his guitar. I could hear his pungent music even climbing the stone steps to the Hoenirs' floor and pushing through the thronged hallway, before I'd entered the open door of the apartment.

My eyes found Hoenir's wife first, by the window, the top of her tawny head like fire on the sun, her chin tilted high, staring raptly at the ever-whispering lips of grayhaired fiftyish Count Daon d'Quaosaont—though I didn't know his name then. Soon I learned his name; later I discovered his gambit; much later I came upon how his ancestor Count Laon had earned their title during the days of the Monarchy before Reupeo became a Republic, though now Count Daon owned two or three motorcar dealerships, a lot of land, and Smepriroa's professional soccer squad.

In any case, Freddi Hoenir had her irongreen eyes fixed on Count Daon's face, listening to him so intently that I decided to wait to give her the six straw coasters I'd bought for her and her husband.

I searched the two rooms for Hoenir, but couldn't find him, so I poured myself some sweet vermouth, twisted in some lemon and sat down near the guitarist, and where I could take a gander at Freddi Hoenir.

She stood at stiff attention, her feet tight together toed-in, her hips slim and even atop her leanlined legs, her breasts apparent but modestly so; mediumtall inside a little brown velvet dress; her arms bare, relaxed, but one cold hand steadily turning like a bolt worn of threading, her yellowgold wedding ring. Count Daon ever secure in his pedigree, whispered on.

And still no sign of Hoenir.

About six, after Count Daon kissed her hand, a gesture she accepted stoically while taking the crisp white card he pressed into her palm, bid her good evening, and made his exit, Freddi Hoenir walked straight over to me. "Don't think I didn't see you come in, Chig Dunford."

I wished her a happy anniversary and gave her the coasters.

"Isn't that nice of you." She didn't open the package, continued to stare at me. "I dare you to have an adultery with me, Chig Dunford."

"Why?" I asked, surprised.

"That's what John would've said. God I wish I'd said that."

What had she wished she had said? I asked, thoroughly confused.

"Why. I wish I'd said 'why.' " She paused in thought. "Have you seen my husband yet?"

I shook my head, but offered to help her find him.

"Thank you, Chig Dunford." She gripped my wrist, leaned her lips close to my ear. "Could I ask you then please to run cross the Beulward to the Cafe of One Hand—do you know it?—and fetch John home to our party."

I left immediately, and though the cold started at five thirty in September, found Hoenir at a sidewalk table, by the soft light of the streetlamps, writing in his speckled notebook. I approached the table, waited to speak until he reached the end of a sentence.

"Hey, kid." Hoenir smiled tiredly. "Sit down. The break'll do me good. I got stuck. I should've started this chapter yesterday when I felt hot. Just a couple of sentences to prime me. Trying to describe how it feels to wake up in a strange bed. See what I mean? You wake up in a strange bed, in a strange room, maybe from a strange dream, then you realize where . . ."

He paused; I told him his wife had sent me for him.

"The party. I almost forgot." He closed his eyes a minute. "But I got to finish this page or I'll fall behind." He opened his eyes, explained. "I started working at six this morning. I already started this page twenty times. If I stop now without finishing the page, I just wasted a day out of my life. Get my point? So do me a favor, kid. Please. Go tell Freddi you couldn't find me. I got to keep writing . . .

OCTOBER
1964

time in October because on that occasion Hoenir happened to express some very provocative opinions on the subject of sex:

"Sex time for fun, kid, equals wasted time."

At first I didn't believe he meant it; he'd never seemed particularly puritanical before that.

"Puritanical? Not me. Anyone can do anything with anyone, I don't give a shit. But as far as I control what I do with my time, I say sex time goes right down the drain. Except if you want a kid. And right now I don't."

But surely he overstated his opinions for dramatic effect, I told him.

"Listen, kid, you ever really think about screwing—as a time-consuming activity? Imagine if you had to describe screwing to someone off a saucer from space. He'd ask you why you do it; you'd mention procreation. Then he'd ask you if you did it for any other reason. You wouldn't say you did it for fun. For love or money, sure. For fun, never."

I mumbled something about many people seeming to have fun when they did it.

"Looked that way to you, kid? You saw any people screwing lately? In the flesh?"

I confessed I'd never actually seen people doing it.

"I saw a screwing show south of the border one time, but that was a show. Real people but on a stage. Not real people in real bedrooms. So who knows who's having fun? Besides, after you put your clothes back on, what do you get? Nothing. Both parties just let a load of time go down the drain." Hoenir turned to look out of the dirtsmeared window of the train we rode northeast into the foothills surrounding Smepriroa, heading toward the Reupeon country town of Conopeursa, where each October the townsmen held a Carnival to commemorate and celebrate the conversion, nine hundred years earlier, of their ancestors to Christianity.

I'd only heard about the Carnival that morning when Hoenir came pounding on my door at seven thirty. After I'd opened up to him, he ordered me to dress at once or we'd miss the train which left Smepriroa's terminal at eight fifteen for Conopeursa.

Hoenir said he'd gotten up at five to finish his page so he could come for me. "The old guy who told me about it says the Carnival lasts all day with parades, pageants and parties from dawn til tomorrow dawn—a real blast."

But I couldn't go; I had tickets for that afternoon on a flight to Paris.

"Hey, kid, you can go to Paris or Rome or Berlin anytime. But you could live your whole life and never get a second chance to see this Carnival. Besides, I feel like talking to somebody on the train; Freddi drove up last night with the Count."

Hoenir meant Count Daon d'Quaosaont; who'd promised to meet him at the Conopeursa station and drive Hoenir to the Villa d'Quaosaonts for lunch before Hoenir, his wife and Count Daon returned to town for the Carnival.

Count Daon, however, did not meet the train; we waited in the station for half an hour, then woke up a driver asleep in his ancient hearselike taxi and bounced higher into the hills surrounding Conopeursa, a cluster of cutstone cottages with reddish roofs crouched under the pale autumn sun.

We entered the dark woods, came up to the bonewhite mansion in a clearing half the size of a football field with a mountain stream tearing through its back gardens, and Count Daon's silvergray Fafaleo parked in the curving drive leading to the villa's front portico.

As our driver braked to a halt, Count Daon and Freddi Hoenir emerged from the mansion onto the marble portico, he in gray slacks and shooting jacket with a pocket for shotgun shells over his heart, she in a brown Glen plaid skirt and rust-colored sweater set, her tawny hair in pigtails sticking from under a black felt polo helmet.

She waved to us from the portico, but Count Daon alone approached our taxi, inspected Hoenir, me, then Hoenir again. "Morning, John. Seems the train made good time."

Hoenir looked at the watch on his wrist. "It took two and a half hours. We got tired waiting for you, Count, so we rented a taxi. Did we miss anything?"

Count Daon squinted slightly. "Nothing, my boy."

"Great!" Hoenir smiled, remembered me. "Hey, meet Chig Dunford."

"Yes." Count Daon flared his nostrils. "Morning."

"Hey, Count, tell Freddi to come over—"

"That wouldn't be advisable, John. We're leaving now and you can talk to her when you next see her. You'll follow, of course." In a dialect of Reupeonese I couldn't understand, he gave our driver some instructions, nodded to us and returned to Freddi Hoenir who'd meanwhile taken a seat in his Fafaleo. Count Daon climbed in beside her, started the engine—

disappeared through the driveway arch before our driver shifted gear.

Hoenir didn't seem to notice. As the driver carried us back to town, he resumed his monologue on sex.

"Wait until you get married, kid, and can screw anytime you want, in a bed, with no one looking to catch and punish you. You get so used to doing it, you ask yourself strange questions at strange times: Why do I do this thing I did so many times before when I really want to do something I never did before? Hell, I'd rather write than screw anytime. I'd rather spend time talking to a pretty girl than screwing her. I'd rather talk to an old woman than screw a pretty girl. I'd rather talk to the oldest man in the world than screw the prettiest woman.

"You take this Count Daon. Freddi brought him home one night for supper after her riding. At first he didn't look like too much, but that old guy can talk. He talks better than I write, and he's lived through more stories than I wrote yet. You can do a lot of stuff in fiftyfive years in Reupeo, and I bet if we asked him he'd say he didn't spend even as few as 366 hours a year of that time screwing. One hour a day in a leap year!

"Okay, I stay on the safe side and give it one hour each and every day, except when it's raining. The other twentythree hours, I try not to think about sex at all."

Soon we again reached Conopeursa. The driver took what seemed like a purposeless route through a maze of narrow streets clogged with celebrating Conopeursans and their gawking, camera-clicking visitors. At least three parades marched at once, each trumpeting and drumming a different set of tunes. The marchers in the first parade wore boots and furs, their faces painted blue. Another parade, musicians and marchers alike, wore black robes flowing below ash-grayed faces. A third contingent, in redface, wore armor, carried axes. All groups marched as if by whim, at times one passing another going opposite ways.

After carrying us in a circle or two around the town's central castle, our driver pulled up to the railway station and parked in exactly the same spot where we'd found him earlier. Across the plaza fronting the station, the clock over the doorway of the Office of Authority read one o'clock.

The driver slid open his window, his bulbous eyes bright, and spoke in Reupeonese: "Thus, my sirs, your visit to the hill country where you witnessed the Carnival in Conopeursa comes to a close, with just enough time remaining for you to buy a postcard or trinket at the stand in the station before the train for Smepriroa arrives."

Hoenir stared at me, waiting I realized for a translation; I repeated the driver's farewell speech.

"Hey, but what about the Count and Freddi?" Hoenir blinked. "Didn't the Count tell him where to take us?"

The driver smiled, explained to me in Reupeonese that he understood English, but could speak only a few phrases of it. In any case, he continued, Count Daon had given his usual instructions; to show the man the town, then put him on the next train for Smepriroa. "His Authority gives usually this command, as if a tour of Conopeursa, even on the hallowed day of the Carnival, would compensate the cuckold for—" The driver trailed off, sighed, frowned.

I hesitated to translate that, but reading Hoenir's face, realized he'd grasped the thrust of the driver's remarks. He stared at me for a long moment, as if waiting to see my reaction first, then snorted. "So that makes Count Daon quite a snatch-hound."

"If I understand, yes, my sir," the driver said in Reupeonese directly to the blankfaced Hoenir. "All over Europe as well as in your own country, His Authority Count Daon d'Quaosaont has worked to earn himself a reputation as one of our epoch's great seducers, specializing in rich married women. No, my sir, do not believe yourself the first husband to see our Carnival through the tears of shame and rage."

Hoenir looked at me. "This guy's lost me again, kid."

I asked Hoenir what he wanted to do.

He thought, looked at his corduroy pants. "Hell, I came up here to see a Carnival, so bring it on!"

On my face Hoenir saw that his misfortune troubled me.

"Hey, kid, don't worry about Freddi. I married Freddi seven years one month six days two hours and five minutes ago." He sighed, seemed relieved. "Let someone else run it for a while."

Hoenir had me ask the driver how much we owed him; not a reupeo, came the reply. On all such occasions, Count Daon paid a fixed sum for the day, forty reupeos, four dollars.

When Hoenir heard that, he laughed perhaps too loudly. "That's a good day's wage for Reupeo. At least she didn't chase off with a miser."

The driver, who'd heard and understood, volunteered to take us on the real tour of the real attractions of the real Conopeursa on the hallowed day of the Carnival. Hoenir accepted his offer.

The first thing then, according to the driver, the three of us had to get euphorically intoxicated. "Only then, my sirs, can we truly experience the deep emotions throbbing within the hearts of the townsmen of Conopeursa on this hallowed day."

He squeezed his taxi through the packed streets, into crammed backstreets, braked finally and parked in front of a blacksmith shop, his cousin's place of work. We climbed out, went inside, passing around the forge banked low for the time being, and out into a back court, open to the sky with gnarled bare trees and shrubbery, which concealed the entrance to a small cave.

In that cave, we found a dozen men sitting in a circle on rocks, beercrates or boxes, taking swallows in turn from a goat-skin flask of VeurNoveurna (OldNinety), an illegal brew.

And from this point on, Hoenir's and my adventures in Conopeursa, which ended hours later after a donkey-cart ride back to my room in Smepriroa, became an amber-filtered, licorice-flavored blur. OldNinety. When the driver said euphorically intoxicated, he meant business. Smooth? I tasted real Irish whisky one Christmas Eve and I remember the smoothness of it, but OldNinety tasted more smooth and more light, glowing amber like brandy, but tasting like licorice, and smooth.

Old: because Conopeursans brewed and drank it in worship of their pre-Christian gods; Ninety: because alcohol composes ninety percent of it, but smooth. OldNinety is fantastic!

It just lifted us off the ground. When we left the cave the first time, the taxi rode like an airplane above the mostly unpaved streets of Conopeursa. The driver took us all over town, then brought us back to the courtyard, the cave, the men and OldNinety.

Much later, when OldNinety had turned us friendly and honest, the driver in his fractured English remarked that he admired Hoenir's reaction to his torment.

Some had made the mistake of challenging Count Daon to a duel, for which not a few paid with their lives usually as a result of massive internal bleeding; Count Daon when challenged always chose Staves. (One could duel to death in Reupeo if one registered beforehand with the Office of Authority.) But Hoenir, to translate the driver's idiomatic expression, had not licked egg off his nose, letting his woman go to the castle as in the days of the Monarchy when all women belonged to the aristo—

"Hey, kid, turn this guy off." Hoenir knit his brows in a mockfrown, winked at me. "So I shrugged and walked away; no big deal.

"Because sitting here with you guys thinking about me and Freddi, I can see things clear. Okay, I didn't have any money, just a college degree. So the heiress from Iowa married the kraut from the Bronx. But I got my points. I know my husbandly duty. So sitting here on this rock, with this flask in my hand, thinking, you know what I figured out?

"In seven years of marriage, I screwed my wife over two thousand times. Now she chases off after this count-guy. Holy cow! That makes her about the most ungrateful piece of snatch on the face of the earth.

"But my time'll come. It'll come right in here." Hoenir tapped his right temple. "Starting to bubble right now. Because this day'll end. And we'll go back to Smepriroa. Or even if we don't. I mean, we will go to sleep somewhere finally tonight. And in the morning, my wrist alarm'll go off, and I don't care where I am, because I got this here." He slapped the speckled notebook in the pocket of his Harris tweed sports jacket. "Wherever I wake up, I'll wash my face, and drink some coffee black, and start turning part of my life into one page of prose fiction . . .

NOVEMBER
1964

time we have before you leave to clarify my portrait of him because one could easily assume that Hoenir let Count Daon d'Quaosaont steal his wife and did nothing about it but get himself looped. Eventually Hoenir did challenge Count Daon to a duel, though the challenge and duel took place in November, a full month following the Carnival at Conopeursa.

In the meantime, I'd finally gotten to Paris, where I stayed about three weeks, searching for old friends, and meeting many glorious places again.

One morning a week after I'd returned to Smepriroa, I met Hoenir at the Cafe of One Hand. We talked over coffee. He told me he'd just started to finish the book he'd begun the Monday morning after the Assassination. I asked him if he had a title for it.

"Knew the title the day I started it, *Dan Hanover*. It's about the death of my innocence." He poked me with his elbow. "I guess."

A few afternoons later he came to my room (I didn't have a phone; few did in Smepriroa) to invite me out to dinner. He'd just sold a story to *MUFF* magazine, written years before, he told me, about a picnic that turned into a manhunt; and he wanted to celebrate. "So come on, kid, you can order anything you want. My treat."

My Paris jaunt had exhausted my resources; my cupboard held but one can of sardines, two water crackers, some coffee and a half litre of wine; thus, though I had much reading to do for my thesis, with pleasure I accepted Hoenir's invitation.

Outside the cold rain poured straight down from the dark-gray sky. In November in Smepriroa, the sun sets at three. Hoenir and I walked out my street to Beulward dol Touras, then up the hill toward a cheerful, clean, cheap restaurant we knew, the sound of rain on my army-surplus parkahood drowning thought.

Hoenir as always wore neither coat over his Harris tweed jacket nor hat on his sandyhaired head. He told me once he enjoyed the cold, and he seemed to ignore the wet.

But I felt miserable; when we reached Lua Greurnda (The Big) Cafe, Smepriroa's largest and most fashionable, I requested that we step inside for a nip of something warming.

Hoenir gave my upper arm a punch, rain spattering his fist. "Sure, kid. Maybe they got some OldNinety stashed."

The rainy days of November drove the natives into Smepriroa's cafes; we found Lua Greurnda crammed, the air heavy with cigarette smoke and wine-coated conversation, steam frosting its high, wide plate glass windows.

We walked up and down the aisles of round tables and wirework chairs looking for a place to sit until quite unexpectedly, Hoenir's eye fell upon the form of Count Daon d'Quaosaont sitting at a table in the Nobility Enclosure, the section of Lua Greurnda that the café's management, in keeping with the custom of Reupeo, reserves for that Republic's still powerful hereditary aristocracy.

Not the sight of Count Daon, but rather the presence of his female companion (an older, more classically beautiful woman than Hoenir's wife, and wearing a wedding band), made the writer march into the Nobility Enclosure to issue his challenge, he later explained. "Imagine a guy robs you, then makes you look when he bums your money. I had loads of bad gas to blow off the second I saw him with that dame. So you saw me, kid, I just walked up to his table, set on making him lose his temper."

Having endured many such situations already in his life, Count Daon remained calm. "Very well, John. But let me say I accept your challenge with reluctance. I'd thought our friendship equal to any stress a woman's irrationality might put to it." Count Daon drew a deep breath. "I choose Staves, John. How's tomorrow at ten? I'll send a motorcar round for you and your second (Dunsford, is it?) at nine. I know a well-kept Staves-Pitch just several kilometers beyond Citygates. On the way, I'll stop to register our names at the Office of Author—"

"But what about now, Count? Step outside with me a couple minutes. I don't want a real duel, just to blow off some bad gas."

Count Daon snorted, glancing at the steam-gilded expanse of Lua Greurnda's window. "John, my boy, can't you see it's raining?"

Hoenir shifted his weight, one foot to the other. "Don't tell me you're afraid of a little rain, Count."

Count Daon frowned. "Much as I hate to appear inflexible about the Ways of Staves, John, I'll remind you that custom dictates that a Match take place the morning following the day the challenge's been offered. Furthermore, you challenged.

Having choice of weapons, and dwelling in ignorance of boxing, I chose Staves. But not to fret; I shall gauge the quality of hurt you'll receive so to punish you sufficiently but no more, for what you've done to your wife."

Hoenir backed up a step, his shoulders hunched as if he had pistols to draw. "What do you mean what I done?"

"Why, you've taken a lovely girl and in seven years, you've ravaged and ruined her." Count Daon lowered his voice. "She told me everything, but because I've known Frederica most of her life, one quick glance told me the full story of her seven-year ordeal." He turned to his companion, whose olive-hued oval face had remained so still I hadn't known if she understood English. "And she'd seemed a perfectly cunning child. I'd met her when her father served here in some diplomatic capacity after the War."

The woman smiled slightly.

Count Daon shook his head in sadness, fixed Hoenir with a disapproving gaze. "No, John, the girl's a burnt-out case, and one must assume her years with you—"

"Hey listen, I'm a good husband," Hoenir asserted. "Touching all bases, starting with, I love my wife."

"How quaint that even the New World's men, old as well as young, continue to cling to the idea that love means everything, or for that matter, anything.

"Perhaps you do love your wife, John, but that certainly hasn't kept you from abusing her shamefully." Count Daon waved Hoenir out of his sight. "Til tomorrow at ten then."

"You old fart—who do you think you fool with that routine, flicking your fingers at me like a queen instead of a count?

"I'm not naive like my wife, who spent most of her childhood in a little town her father happened to own. I grew up in the Bronx, the only borough of New York City on the mainland of the American continent, and that means I saw one of you anytime I snuck on the subway and went to hang around one of those big hotels. Your stuff doesn't impress me; I seen screwballs and sliders before this. Just show me proper respect or I'll serve your false teeth to you on a tray and embarrass you in front of this new piece of snatch you're sticking it into! And by the way, where did you say Freddi is?"

Count Daon's face turned scarlet, slowly reddening as he rose from his seat. "I didn't—John, you've been unforgivably disrespectful to your elders and betters; I see I can't wait til tomorrow to teach you your lessons."

"Great! So you finally decided to step outside and let a little rain drop on your precious skull." Hoenir started to dance in tight circles on the toes of his white tennis shoes. "I can see what you mean about Freddi being burnt-out, except it might surprise you to know I saw that on my first date with her. But I married her anyway. So you can't really blame me for that. And I can't really blame you, because if not you, then some guy. But Holy cow! Count, you pretended to be my friend—that's the bad gas that is really between us. But we'll punch around awhile, then have a few drinks and I'll feel squared up with you."

His face still glowing red above his white starched collar, Count Daon summoned the waiter; sent him scurrying for the manager of Lua Greurnda, who arrived in another minute, his small dry hands washing themselves with each other.

"Bring the Staves!" Count Daon commanded.

The manager's little round face went chalky; he gulped, then clapped his hands twice, and the corps of waiters set frantically to work transforming the Nobility Enclosure of Lua Greurnda into a Staves-Pitch.

After politely reseating around the perimeter of the enclosure those members of the nobility in attendance that evening, the waiters cleared the area, stacking tables and chairs neatly in the enclosure's four corners.

Next, they tossed down enough fresh sawdust to cover and dry both the tile floor and the wet sawdust they'd tossed down that morning to staunch the tide of the November rains. Last, the tuxedoed headwaiter wheeled in from the kitchen on a serving cart an iron washtub filled to the brim with a bed of red-hot charcoal. Using stout detachable handles, the waiters set this tub of coals upon the floor in the center of the enclosure, and the headwaiter dropped onto the ember bed several pieces of raw wood, which flared into flame, crackling, running sap, filling Lua Greurnda with the campfire scent of pine.

Meanwhile, the manager of Lua Greurnda had hurried away to his office, to return shortly carrying across his forearms an old but lovingly preserved case of brown leather, resembling a flute case but something over a yard long, and opening at one end. This case contained the Staves.

In truth, I learned I'd seen Staves often before. Each brown-uniformed National Policeman carried one, only the Nationals paint theirs white, which makes it difficult to discern the weapon's distinctive shape.

It measures exactly three feet long and at least two feet of its length would pass as ordinary broom handle. The remaining twelve inches, called the stroking end, resembles nothing I've ever seen so much as a long thin thumb, one side round and one side flat, with a slight spoon shape, but carved of hard, lightweight wood; a Stave.

Before the Match began, Count Daon carefully explained the basic Ways of Staves to Hoenir: One had continually to move around the fire, either retreating from or pursuing one's opponent. Each opponent, however, had the right to call two pauses a day to the circuit of the Match, but Count Daon advised Hoenir to save those to relieve himself of wastes; Staves often continued for days and even weeks because usually a Match ended not when one man beat another man senseless, but when one man realized he could not beat the other senseless, that his opponent would rather give up life than speak words of surrender. Most men, rather than kill, left the Staves-Pitch, forfeiting the Match, though occasionally someone died.

"But we won't have any of that here tonight." Count Daon looked for an instant as if he might smile, but didn't. "Let me define the Stroke Zone, John. Strokes above the collarbone as well as below the knee are regarded as ungentlemanly. You must confine your strokes to the torso, hips, buttocks and thighs; and arms of course. Genital strokes are generally regarded as ungentlemanly, though strictly speaking, they fall within the Stroke Zone. In short, if you don't, I shan't." Count Daon cleared his throat with a quiet cough. "Remember, John, in Staves, he who commands the Pitch wins. Defend yourself."

"Defend myself!" Hoenir by now gleefully accepted the idea of a Staves Match with Count Daon. "Me waste my time defending myself?"

The Match began: Hoenir pursued Count Daon around the fire for hours. Count Daon retreated, though never did he show Hoenir his back, around the fire for hours, regulating his retreat to Hoenir's advance, trying, it became obvious, to keep the fire between them.

At times during the early hours of the Match, Hoenir might add an extra effort to his rush, breaking within stave-length of Count Daon—to receive a stave tongue in the pit of his stomach, a backarm stroke to his exposed lower ribs, a chop across the top of his thighs, a broad stroke to his buttocks. With Hoenir stung and befuddled, Count Daon would retreat, ever backing up, to the other side of the fire.

Later when pain had slowed Hoenir's pursuit of him to a dreary trudge, Count Daon took the opportunity of relaxed pace to take a morsel of bread and cheese offered by the manager of Lua Greurnda, or a glass of amber-colored wine from his still-silent female companion.

Staves may not sound like much compared to quickly completed games like football, hockey, boxing or rugby, but then only I saw the blue bruises on Hoenir's buttocks, washed the white scorchlike scars covering his hips and ribs, smeared salve on the red welts rising out of his sunstarved skin from his knees to his chest and back. But I'll spare us the gruesome details. I'll just say that Count Daon d'Quaosaont continually in retreat poked, chopped, paddled, pummeled and prodded John Hoenir's torso one notch short of bloody.

After seven hours Count Daon ended the Match; and I supported a barely conscious Hoenir out of Lua Greurnda through the rain to a taxi, got him home and up the stairs to his apartment cold and damp, now in the November rains, and without his wife there, no good reason to keep the gas heater going. I undressed and cleaned him up, helped him on with his pajamas, into bed, then made him some packaged soup, finally took the bowl from his lap when he'd fallen to sleep.

I tried to sleep on the couch in the livingroom. Outside, the rain still rained; the temperature had dropped to thirty-three. Once or twice I heard Hoenir groan, waited for him to call out, but he kept silence. He had never complained of pain, but I had seen it burning inside him through his eyes.

Finally I did drift off to sleep; to awake soon after dawn wondering how the cold rain could make so much noise, clattering as if falling through a hole in the roof into twentysix pie pans. But Hoenir's roof didn't have a hole that big.

I opened my eyes and listened, then sat up, watching my breath steaming the damp chilly air of Hoenir's apartment. I shivered as my ear separated the cold sizzle of the everfalling November rain from the clatter and chatter of John Hoenir's typewriter . . .

DECEMBER
1987

time this morning the postman brought a novel entitled *Dan Hanover,* the work of a writer I met during the years I spent studying and traveling in Reupeo. Perhaps you've heard mention of his name: John Hoenir; published his short fiction in some of the nation's finest magazines, including *Toast*; *Bicker's Weekly*; *MUFF: The Gothamerican*. But then, like me, you probably remember the plots of the stories you read in magazines, but forgot the name of the author before you've followed the continuations through to the back pages.

In any case, Hoenir had his editor send me his novel, a thoughtful gesture. Because I haven't heard or read a word from him since the last time I set eyes on him in Smepriroa's massive railroad terminal, nine in the morning of New Year's day, many years ago in December 1964, though his niece went here briefly in the late 1970s.

We'd just returned from his wife's parents' chalet in the Reupeon Alps, forty hours of uncomfortable travel in a frigid drafty boxcar with benches, not counting the mountain train, punctuated finally by Hoenir's abrupt farewell: "Hey, kid, seeyaround!"

He'd given me his glacierwide smile, punched my breastbone, slapped his speckled notebook through his sportcoat pocket—disappeared into the passing throngs.

And this morning his book appeared unautographed. I sat right down and started to read it. I didn't have any papers to correct or lectures to prepare; I had only to wait for you to arrive. I got reading it just as you knocked. See it there? He completed the first draft of it on that trip to the Reupeon Alps I mentioned. We'd boarded the train in Smepriroa at four in the afternoon, and talked til midnight.

Exhausted by the rush of packing—Hoenir had burst into my room at three, saying that his wife demanded that he bring me to a New Year's Eve party in a chalet in Laokeurbedaon, a combination health spa and ski resort in the Reupeon Alps—and the agonies of the eight hours we'd already traveled, and despite the cold, I fell asleep.

When I woke I found Hoenir at work his nose steaming in the freezing car, his speckled notebook open on his knees; pen filling paper with blue ink. For a moment he paused to report:

"Going hot, kid. Only 6:37 and already I got seventyfive words of the last page of the first draft of my first novel." He returned to his work, but before he'd finished we arrived at Breurge, where we changed to a local railway that ran a train of compartments most way up the mountain that Laokeurbedaon sat atop.

As we climbed and Hoenir worked I watched the wind whisk snow off gleaming peaks; we wound even higher—tilting level ultimately, one hundred yards later the train sighing to a halt in a wooden station as brittle and quaint as a snowflake magnified.

"Holy cow . . ." The train lurched to a standstill; Hoenir looked up, his brown eyes filled with pure wonder. "I finished it."

I offered my congratulations.

He nodded, closed the notebook. "I thought I'd never reach the end." He stood up, stretched, slid his book into his pocket, and opened the door of our woodpaneled compartment. "Come on, kid. I know the way. We'll hike it."

I donned my parka, took down my suitcase and followed Hoenir out of the station and through the village; a butchery, a bakery, a wheelchair store and two new ski shops.

Up there the air seemed so clean and clear that it rang, but through my nylon socks and oxfords, the frozen mountain numbed my feet.

We reached the outskirts of the village in ten minutes, continued climbing the frozen road toward a jerry-built chalet of lacquered pine with a steepslant roof the same shade blue as the sky.

Fifty yards from the chalet, Hoenir stopped so I could catch up. "Hey, kid, let me sketch in this scene for you. Freddi called yesterday morning, the first time I even knew where she was since October. She said if I wanted her again, I should come here, and I should bring you." For a moment he looked away to the white mountain spires, ledges of rock snowtopped, looming above the village. "I don't know definitely what she has on her mind, I guess she wants you to chaperone us while we talk it over. But I'll square with you; I hope I get some snatch in the next couple of days. I deserve some. I just as good as finished my first novel."

Now that he'd fulfilled his wife's request to bring me, I told him, he could forget about me; in my suitcase I carried three thick books I had to read in preparation for my thesis on Dupukshamin.

"Hey, don't get me wrong. Freddi means more to me than just the snatch. I missed her." He whispered, his words almost lost in the cold air, then snorted steam. "But you don't know anything about missing someone. You never got married yet."

He turned and marched on to the chalet, up a stone stairway to a small green door, calling his wife. "Hey, Freddi! Open up! I just got in! Freddi? Hey, open up!"

I tried to keep pace with him, but found the going difficult because of the suitcase I lugged along the ice-slick roadway under my blazingcold feet.

When she opened the door, Freddi Hoenir seemed already to understand my distress, ignored her husband's smile to skip down the stairs and greet me. "Chig Dunford, so good to see you again. Did you bring warm socks?"

I rested my suitcase, shaking my head.

"Your poor feet must be stiff. Didn't John mention the cold?"

I shook my head again. "Hello, Freddi. Nice to—"

But she'd turned to stare up the stone steps at Hoenir. "John, when will you learn to consider other people?"

Hoenir smiled innocently. "To consider other people what?"

She sighed, stooped to heft up my suitcase with her right hand, and leaning way to her left, carried it up the steps, passing Hoenir, and into the chalet. Hoenir followed her inside.

I caught up to them in the chalet's livingroom; lowceilinged and cozy, warmed toasty by a large square oven jutting from most of one wall, and over two hundred years old according to the date cast into its iron door.

A large oval table and six chairs around it filled most of the room, leaving just enough space for a large round girl with big blue eyes and sprayset blond hair, draped in a black billowy silken gown, and seated in a leather chair. Her face, as large as a dinner plate, she'd hidden behind the smaller hand-painted mask of a coquette, her neck of many chins wrapped with a dozen glittering necklaces, her small hands encrusted with rings.

Freddi Hoenir introduced us and she, Gunhild Buster (I believe), extended her hand to me. I took it, felt her desires transmitted through the flesh of my palm straight to my fluttering heart.

"Gunhild makes films," Freddi Hoenir explained.

Gunhild kept my hand. "If you'll seat yourself and let me remove your shoes, I'll warm your feet and tell you the whole story. You'll relish the tale, I promise."

Freddi Hoenir answered for me. "Chig Dunford thinks you've had a lovely idea, Gunhild." She pinched Hoenir's sleeve and led him from the room. "Come, John, we have the sleeping arrangements to discuss." Through the wall, I heard them climbing stairs to the chalet's upper floor. Gunhild still had not released my hand; my back hurt; I couldn't stand up straight. I tried to ease my hand out of hers, but she wouldn't let go, her rings grinding my knuckles. Instead she began to pull me downward until I had bent to a bow, my nose only inches from hers, our gazes locked.

"Got anything against group grope, Chig Dunford?" she asked.

"Excuse me?" I replied.

"I should hope not; why do you suppose we invited you?" She loosened her grip in bewilderment.

I pulled my hand away, stood up, spine popping, and told her I believed I'd received an invitation in order to act the chaperone to the Hoenirs.

"Chaperone!" she howled. "What exactly did you believe you could keep them from doing?"

I shivered. "You know . . . sleeping together . . ."

"But of course we will, all of us, me, you, Frederica, the whole—"

"Piece of snatch went freaky!" Opening the door, Hoenir slammed it into the iron oven. "Hey, Chig, let's head back to Smepriroa."

Nodding, I picked up my suitcase from where Freddi Hoenir had placed it in a corner of the room, and we started back to Laokeurbedaon's quaint railway depot, arriving just minutes before the train of compartments began backing down the mountain to Breurge.

Hoenir talked all the way: "Tell you about me, Chig. Basically I like to sleep alone. My parents only had me so I always had my own bed. Just me in my own bed in my own room, like that for my first eighteen years on earth.

"Then I went away to college, the first time in my life assigned a roommate, who became my friend. I ever tell you about Denn? They found him dead. Everyone said he bumped himself off. But he got murdered, because he learned something—remind me to tell you the story sometime . . .

"Anyway, I finally married Freddi, the first time in the twentytwo years I lived so far that I had to share a bed with somebody. Every night. Listen kid, you got that to look forward to: each time you move you run into a knee or an elbow or something you don't quite recognize by touch. In the beginning, I woke up three times a night, wondering who kept doing all the shoving, because it takes a couple of seconds to remember when you wake up that you got married. Then I'd see this little piece of snatch taking up all the space, sprawling from one corner of the bed to the other.

"But I got used to it, came to like the ear handy at night when I wanted to talk. I decided being married liberated me; I didn't have to think about every new piece of snatch I just saw. I had my own at home. What did I care for all that snatch choking the sheets. Then—clack!—the blinkers came off. I could see women as people. And you know something? The greatest women make terrible people! Men make much better people than women anytime. You want to know Freddi's trouble? She wants to be a person. But a woman can't be a person. Only a man can be a person. But he better be a man first."

Hoenir shook his head and sighed. "She did some strange things before, but I guess she'll get over this too, though I don't know how she could think I'd want to waste my time, fast as life goes by, doing something useless such as bringing in the New Year in a feather bed with her, a fat lady, you and a pack of people I didn't meet yet!"

I tried to stifle my chuckle but failed.

"Get my point? Holy cow, wait until I tell the Count about what that snatch tried to get me to do! But I guess he's seen some pretty freaky stuff in his time."

I asked him if he meant Count Daon d'Quaosaont.

Hoenir nodded. "We get together once or twice a week. He teaches me the Ways of Staves." He punched my shoulder across the compartment. "Hey, next time we go out to the Staves-Pitch, we'll stop by for you . . ." But as I say, I haven't seen John Hoenir since we parted company next morning at the railroad terminal in Smepriroa.

At first I almost felt snubbed when he didn't come to fetch me. But then, what reason had I to feel snubbed? The Ways of Staves, the martial arts in general, didn't light fires in my imagination. Too much fighting in the world anyway. And Hoenir knew it. I had already declined to fight him once.

Eventually, I learned to accept the supposed snub as a contradictory compliment. Understanding that I had my thesis to complete, Hoenir hadn't wanted to waste my time, or his own; and time, of course, he valued above money.

"Money you got to earn, kid, but time you got to learn," he told me more than once, punching my heart. Time; speaking pseudopoetically, plotting the progress of the person through time possessed him . . .

MAY 1965

SCENE ONE

(The dream. Shadow figures miming actions of voices are heard reading from the following:)

In the mist on the dock an the harbour bay the river around the ighland below the graytestity of the whale Titinac Hold, programing with its very stropheness the pore of Her Stainted Magester, Friginia, her floorashing tredding abyssness in the slunken, soiltry, saveage, stuductive ports of the call, whipped gully its tussles, as if she, three chairs on the old gill, sigg-nalled the larrival upover decks laudy of Lord Limph, Childe d'Lacquedouster, and Amissery Emorable in the Aimpyre's Nervy.

The men asymboled to ear rim constitchuted as sourly an aggressionation of howdy, taphammerfisted, fablefuddled feemen as, keenly, had seen the lee of Siamapurr. Present and prim stood Master Hench, First G'd.Rt.A'm., straight-sucked, stake-sudsed, the only burn seamoan amoon them, a saint asea, but inland an insand stabber of lassoes, scarving up inyards before biling bones in bullyeam (slightly seasoned, sin-ner until croaked).

The causal orbserver might desire to turnderway from both boht and crew at the site of Hitch; but conning his ed, he vood encounter Herr Ehrr, derr Forst Stiward, whein aloofen an oven stouffer, graiduate in veapomcocking from Gurfhousand, one of his two owls putsch-covered. Not tore forget us Gunner Hawnson, not so dippily involved save in Dollarware; or Peat Hyveston, a wooden shoe for a leg-though man to min, measuring measle to pipple, Lurd Lampalot's limes had dumped from Lumdum's lums, by the grave of gunvicted, thence, grumbled off to serve a worm in Her Voyagin Magi'sty's chips. It iwaz on of these—T.Y.S. Woten's Wessel—which Lanece Limp comeondeared.

The herd hord stump-feets from bhelow, and Hack, whip wiping wildely and woundwashed, swabbed the many acidely, making quai for Like Lumanury's uhrival.

Oever, the opening doris had revealed the sprightly brittle Benyangian boatboy, Bo Changles, a kwute waddle fellow with a ponepensity to expand within his kneebreetches and wastecoat, though when Load Loom speared him in a tokenboat through the pocket mirror one aftemoird off the cusp of Ymomsamaman, he looked depositively all thin.

Teeny, a baby he in fact washed (not at all to make a Mose a Morses, though to repose the poseabilities of dustituation, he could bring them the beat in a certain water down the ways, jes us like Sangmonde Froid cooled the Allemammer team, 4–1 minute's time, though kneed alltimetely by Audolf and his tiwas yochling odors) and bathed him in snow hite, lining the cellar plyroom with pictures of him being good, beng bagd but in all ways keeping him emported in the footlockers at the ankle of his brain.

Lynmp hoped, as he remarked it ti Rudderwick of Venice, Whaler like himself, that, as his aid, regarding less of his slumming list of wit, and of certain faciel complexionities—his nose of run, his lip of skin, his overall greasy, Hugh-ear—the little pickapeppa would turn an Enguishman yet, as Gode as many of your Tigs, Dains or Harald Femirs.

But Hak had ever stoked a stomp on Chaggle's bow. "Spades, Beamish, if we went wind-up without warrant."

"Don't worry, Mr. Phox. He'll come up in a mienute," Choke ashored deminimem.

Hick steifled his aarrm, prepared to rook Chick's nag. "Be thee without mannerisms of pealty? Where's yee servience when you dress Master Hex?"

Chaca chivaled. "Come on, my sir, be you, man."

"Humunhuh?"

"Hoosee! What are you doe-wing with this weet title laddie?" Fore indood, Laimpule had skippled upon deck, his cuttles slient, his heels hispy. "Don't you know this is my personel savant? Come a her, sun."

Chag mated his ground, resighing about time, shoking the head's world.

"Coma to me, Chookie. I've bought a surprise for you. Calm on out, Wedely-dear."

The hubburb doors slidely soapened to a russelle of sulk powdering a poute, a furdrove fuller bushes, a pinpint of ladderpadder cheetihose, sverevel knocky neezen, two fletschy shudderblades, one large wopfer in the middle, a petipilvis off to one side and no whitter than a pain of window, glassblyeyes calling to mine the chillchurls of the House of Assguard. "Heelo, Chit."

But that whooshn't his windy near as he could reember her, though he knew its suckled meaning.

"Ates this? A wruinman abroad?" Hache, taking two fresh chups from the norest swale, pounded Limp's boff, handsiftedly. "Rag nor rocker headed if he torches haarr!"

"Thanks, but I don't want chees in fish."

"Lamplear, tele Hunch to shut up." She beered her teesks. "I wamp the chigger, Daddy, eight inch to bar. Wheely."

"Miss Chill? Pardon me, but—"

Whapt snacked Haunch's scatterninetails. "I bliv yiv bid tiribly inviting this Ifrikin tithy pirty."

"I want you. Holy." Talonese fingersnails pierced his ear, hire breathsts in his face. "Golly me, Wole."

(Dream sequence fades.)

SCENE TWO

(In the cabin. WALLY and LYNN are on the bottom bunk. CHIG is on the top.)

LYNN
I want you, Wally.

WALLY
Sure, Lynn. But not now, I mean, I think he's up there.

LYNN
Well?

(CHIG checks his watch.)

WALLY
What do you want to do?

LYNN
I want you, Wally. Now.

WALLY
With him up there? He might wake up.

LYNN
Oh, Wally. I'm really upset with you, Wally.

WALLY
But we can't just, you know . . . Golly, with him up there? We can wait until he goes out.

LYNN
When does he go out?

WALLY
I don't know. When he wakes up.

LYNN
Why don't you wake him up and ask him to leave?

WALLY
I hardly know him, Lynn. Besides, you're not even supposed to be here.

LYNN
That's nice, Wally. And you even know what Mr. Oglethrope said.

(CHIG rolls over in bed.)

WALLY
Lynn? He's waking up.

LYNN
Shhh. *(Silence.)* He only turned over. Oh Wally, I want you so bad.

(LYNN begins to kiss WALLY.)

WALLY
Hey! What are you doing?

(LYNN emits a muffled moan, her head under the covers.)

WALLY
Come on, Lynn. Don't do that.

(CHIG rolls back and forth. WALLY and LYNN are quiet for a moment.)

WALLY
He's really waking up.

LYNN
But it's all right now. We can be quiet.

WALLY
Come on, Lynn. Let's go for a swim. Maybe we're missing lunch.

LYNN
You see? He stopped moving. We can be real quiet. You see? Come on, Wally. Really. Really. Wally. Oh, Wally.

(WALLY hums a high tone. CHIG rolls over.)

LYNN
Oh, Wally. Oh, Wally. Oh, golly me, Wally. Golly me. Golly me. Oh. Golly me. Wally. Wally? Oh, Wally. Really? Oh, Wally!

(WALLY is no longer humming.)

LYNN

(Sighing.) Oh, Wally. Why'd you do that?

WALLY

I just couldn't help it. *(Pauses while dressing.)* Are you all right, Lynn?

LYNN

I want a raspberry soda. You think I can have that?

(LYNN and WALLY dress and leave. CHIG climbs down and shrugs. End of scene.)

SCENE THREE

(CHIG and WALLY are on deck.)

WALLY
Get locked out, Mr. Dunford?

CHIG
Yes. How you feeling today, Wally?

WALLY
Great. I made a lot of noise this morning. I hope I didn't wake you.

CHIG
I sleep like a stone, Wally.

WALLY
Great.

CHIG
Well . . .

(WALLY is looking at WENDY, who has just entered on the balcony.)

WALLY
She must be a movie star, huh, Mr. Dunford?

CHIG
Who?

WALLY
Her up there. She's really something.

CHIG
Wow. *(Pause.)* Wendy!

WALLY
(Waving also.) Wendy! *(To CHIG.)* This is great. What movies has she been in? Think you could get her autograph?

WENDY
Why, hello, Chig.

CHIG
How've you been?

WENDY
Well, I'm doing better now.

WALLY
(Overlapping and drowning out WENDY.) Go on ask her, Mr. Dunford. I bet she'll give you one.

CHIG
(To WENDY.) What did you say?

WENDY
I said I'm fine. And would you buy me a drink? *(She nods.)*

CHIG
(Nodding now also.) All right. Where can we meet?

WENDY
The lounge on your deck.

(CHIG stares at WENDY. He does not respond.)

WENDY
Did you hear me? I'll come down there, to the third-class lounge.

CHIG
All right. All right. What time?

WENDY
Four o'clock?

CHIG
Good.

WENDY
See you then.

CHIG
See you, Wendy.

WALLY
She didn't hear you. *(Pause.)* Did you hear me, Mr. Dunford? She didn't hear you.

CHIG
I know.

WALLY
You met her before, Mr. Dunford?

CHIG
(Shaking his head.) I'm not sure, Wally.

WALLY
Huh? *(Pause.)* Hey, you want a drink? Alcohol's real cheap on this boat. Me and my girl got really crashed last night.

CHIG
I didn't know you had a girl, Wally.

WALLY
Sure. We're on the same TYO Tour. We went to the same school, but I didn't meet her until we both happened to be at TYO's Upstate Fun-For-All in Gully City.

CHIG
I didn't know you were on a tour. How many are you?

WALLY
Seventy. Counting Mr. Oglethrope.

CHIG
Seventy? I thought you were travelling alone, Wally.

WALLY
With my Dad? He got real mad when I even first asked him about going to Europe. With TYO. Even though he's in

it. Hey, would you like to meet my girl, just as long as Mr. Oglethrope doesn't catch us?

CHIG
Doing what?

WALLY
Huh? Well, you know about TYO, don't you, Mr. Dunford?

CHIG
Nothing. But they don't want you to drink?

WALLY
Ya, ya no drinking. *(Pause.)* But what I want is for my girl to meet you.

(WALLY begins leading CHIG across deck.)

WALLY
Come on, Mr. Dunford. *(Leading toward the third-class lounge.)* She's mad at me. We had a little spat. And we really shouldn't be talking, but it's real important she gets to meet you.

CHIG
Why me, Wally?

WALLY
Because when we get married, Mr. Dunford, she wants to move East, and I just want her to meet the kind of people she'll meet there.

CHIG

What kind of people, specifically?

WALLY

Huh? Neegro People. I heard the East is full of them, just like you.

(End of scene.)

SCENE FOUR

(LYNN is waiting in the third-class lounge. CHIG and WALLY approach her.)

LYNN
Hi, Wally.

WALLY
Hi, Lynn. You reading?

LYNN
Ya, but I was almost finished.

WALLY
Lynn? I want you to meet the man I live with. Mr. Dunford.

LYNN
I didn't see you. Hi. I'm Lynn.

CHIG
Hello, Lynn.

LYNN
Wally and me had a fight.

CHIG
Yes. Nothing serious, I hope.

WALLY
Sit down, Mr. Dunford, and I'll get some drinks. You want one, Lynn?

LYNN
Liquor, you mean? *(Making a face.)* Are you having one?

WALLY
A little drink never hurt anybody. That's what my Dad says.

LYNN
But Dad Burison doesn't let you drink, Wally.

WALLY
Hell!

LYNN
But you can have a drink if you want, Wally. I didn't say you couldn't.

WALLY
See, Mr. Dunford? She's just like my Mom. She didn't want me to go to Europe either. But Lynn talked her into it.

LYNN

You said you were real glad Mom Burison liked me, Wally. And you wanted to go with TYO too. We both said we'd learn a lot.

CHIG

Wally's probably a little nervous about your fight, Lynn. And he wanted me to meet you. He did, Lynn.

LYNN

I don't know why he feels that way, Mr. Dunford.

WALLY

What way, Lynn? What way? I didn't even say anything.

LYNN

You made me out somebody's mother who ruled them like a queen from the sky.

WALLY

Well, why didn't you let me have one little drink?

LYNN

I turned up my nose because I didn't want one, Wally. You know Mr. Oglethrope said TYO Tour Juniors weren't to be allowed to drink.

WALLY

But he made a lot of other rules too, that you break.

LYNN

You should be real glad—

CHIG
Did you notice, Wally? Everybody's gone.

WALLY
Huh, Mr. Dunford?

(The lounge is empty. It appears that it was abandoned suddenly. Drinks are unfinished and games are left incomplete.)

CHIG
I'll go ask what's going on. I'll be right back.

(CHIG exits. WALLY and LYNN sit in silence for a moment.)

WALLY
Come on, Lynn. Are you gonna stay sore at me?

LYNN
I haven't decided.

WALLY
Couldn't we just kiss and make up?

LYNN
Your friend is coming back.

(They wait in silence as CHIG walks back to the table.)

CHIG
There's a lifeboat drill.

LYNN

It's one-forty already? Mr. Oglethrope'll be really mad at me. We're in the same position, the second-class ballroom.

WALLY

Do we go there too, Lynn?

LYNN

No, Wally, it goes by room. Mr. Oglethrope sleeps across the hall from me.

(LYNN exits.)

SCENE FIVE

(WALLY and CHIG enter a shabby passageway.)

CHIG
Let's forget it, Wally. We're lost.

WALLY
No, really, Mr. Dunford, I know the way.

CHIG
Let's stop, Wally.

WALLY
But we'll miss the drill, Mr. Dunford. If the ship goes down, we'll die.

CHIG
I guess so, but I'm going back to the cabin. All right, Wally?

WALLY
We can open one of these. Maybe there's someone around who can tell us what to do.

(WALLY knocks on the nearest door. He tries opening the door, but it is locked.)

CHIG
I'll see you, Wally.

WALLY
Maybe this door.

(WALLY tries the door and it opens. WALLY and CHIG look into the wings. There are sounds from the room. Stage right we see one African in chains. Behind him, ninetynine slaves in chains.)

WALLY
Huh? Hi. The boiler room?

CHIG
What did they say, Wally?

WALLY
Mr. Dunford? Come here please. Maybe they'll talk to you.

(CHIG moves to the door and looks in. A red glow is coming from the room.)

CHIG
They don't know anything about a lifeboat drill, Wally.

SLAVE
Life bode drill?

CHIG
(Moving closer.) You speak English?

SLAVE
Speaking Franch as well, ndugu? *(Indicating his chains.)* You avez key?

CHIG
But what did you do?

(The slave—and the ninetynine others in the room—laugh.)

SLAVE
Sisi for to make slave.

CHIG
Excuse me?

WALLY
Come on, Mr. Dunford.

(WALLY steps in front of CHIG and pulls the door shut.)

WALLY
Don't pay any attention. They can't help us.

CHIG
Wait a minute. Didn't you hear what he said?

WALLY
Sure, Mr. Dunford. But slavery's been abolished for a hundred years. They're probably just criminals, you know, making a joke.

CHIG
A joke? A joke, Wally?

WALLY
Sure. And we better go before somebody comes. They're probably not allowed visitors. This way, Mr. Dunford.

(End of scene.)

SCENE SIX

(WALLY and CHIG are in the cabin.)

WALLY
It was dirty down there. Did you notice, Mr. Dunford?

CHIG
Can I sit on your bed?

WALLY
Sure, Mr. Dunford. I'm changing my clothes. It was real dirty down there.

CHIG
I'll wait until you leave, then I'll get ready for my date. All right?

WALLY
Huh? Sure, Mr. Dunford. *(Pause.)* I got it. They're sailors who mutinied. Sailors still mutiny, Mr. Dunford. We used to read about them in current events class.

CHIG
But when did they mutiny?

WALLY

Probably a couple days ago.

CHIG

Before we got on the ship?

WALLY

Sure, Mr. Dunford. Why else are they locked up?

CHIG

But didn't you hear . . . He said they were slaves. At least that's what I think he said. I mean, meant.

WALLY

Ya. Maybe that's what you mean, Mr. Dunford. I saw that happen before. We don't like to think about it, but mutineers and people like that are still going around. *(Finishing dressing and snapping to attention.)* Well, I'm ready to go. Do I look all right?

(CHIG points out a protruding handkerchief, which WALLY adjusts.)

WALLY

Thanks, Mr. Dunford. You know, it may sound funny, but sharing this cabin with you has really hit the nail on the head far as my TYO Team Year in Europe is concerned. And thanks for helping me with Lynn.

CHIG

But I don't think I—

WALLY

For talking to her, Mr. Dunford. I knew she'd respect your opinion. You were swell.

(WALLY exits. CHIG remains alone, stunned. Then shouts and pounding begin at the door.)

OGLETHROPE

Wally? Wally? I know you're in there! Come on, Wally! Open up and meet your fate!

(CHIG opens the door. OGLETHROPE enters. He is wearing a giant acorn on a metal chain around his neck.)

OGLETHROPE

Lookout, huh? Where's Wally? I'm Oglethrope.

CHIG

Nice to meet you, Mr. Oglethrope. He just left. You lead the tour he's on, don't you?

OGLETHROPE

Bull's-eye. This Wally's?

(OGLETHROPE pats CHIG's bed. CHIG indicates the other.)

CHIG

My name—

OGLETHROPE

He's been in it every night so far?

CHIG
I think so. Would you like to leave a note for him?

OGLETHROPE
If you want to know the truth, bud, I thought I'd find them right here. Going sneakers.

CHIG
Excuse me?

OGLETHROPE
The both of them. Sneakers. I better not catch them, all I can say. Not that I mind personally. I'm no blankety-blank prude. Going sneakers like that. They signed up knowing the rules. And the rules say no mixing between the sexes.

CHIG
You mean like talking?

OGLETHROPE
You don't know about TYO Team Tours, do you?

CHIG
I've been in Europe, I guess.

OGLETHROPE
You guess? How long do you guess you were there?

CHIG
Eight years. But I was going back and forth. But I think I'm going back for good now.

OGLETHROPE

And tell me, bud, how did you make the money to do this?

CHIG

Scholarships. I was a student.

OGLETHROPE

For eight years? Listen, if you want some friendly advice, you look like a guy at loose ends. When you get to New York, get in touch with your nearest TYO Team Organizer. She could really help you.

CHIG

Excuse me, Mr. Oglethrope, but before I could join TYO, I mean, I'd have to know more about it. I might not even qualify for membership.

OGLETHROPE

Don't worry, bud. We're not like those Eastern clubs. You can join if you get the right frame of mind. Come here.

(CHIG steps away from the door, but leaves it open.)

OGLETHROPE

Come here. Do I look funny to you?

(CHIG shakes his head no.)

OGLETHROPE

At one time, I used to go sneakers, just like them. I was an athlete, you see. I got three pro offers. The night we beat the team from Clearwater, Jerry Orloch bet me five hundred dollars I wouldn't pull out my eye. Well, there was a lot of booze around that night, and I was kidding and he was kidding, but when I started I said to myself, stop when it starts to hurt. But it never did start to hurt. They had to stop me. See for yourself. *(He moves his face close to CHIG's.)*

CHIG

Yes. I . . .

OGLETHROPE

I learned something that night. I was at the bottom of the tree. Wrecked my whole future in sport. The scouts didn't come around anymore. You might think it shames me to tell you something like that, but it doesn't. I get stronger every time I tell it. I know I crashed through with TYO.

CHIG

I guess so.

OGLETHROPE

TYO has representatives in all the hospitals, little women to mend the men and send them back to battle. The Rep at Gully City General was a little cutie of about five foot three. Today that little cutie is called Mrs. Oglethrope.

CHIG

Oh? Is she with the tour?

OGLETHROPE

Not on your life. She's home with my brother, running the store, hardware. You see, TYO taught me that some things are more important than money. Like devotion to duty and sacrifice. Look at all our famous men and the thing that marks them is how much they sacrifice. TYO gave me that. And it can give it to you too. Do me a favor.

CHIG
If I can, Mr. Oglethrope.

OGLETHROPE
Keep an eye on those kids for me. Let me know if you see anything that smells fishy.

CHIG
What do you mean by fishy, Mr. Oglethrope?

OGLETHROPE
Come on, bud. We're all grown-ups here. Just look into Wally's mug, watch him walk. The kid's face is a raspberry bush. Let me have a report at dinner.

CHIG
If I see anything.

(OGLETHROPE exits. CHIG waves as he leaves, then comes back into the cabin. He strips, checks to see if he needs to shave, washes and begins readying for his date as the lights fade. End of scene.)

SCENE SEVEN

(WENDY is seated in the lounge. CHIG enters.)

WENDY
Chig. How are you?

CHIG
Hello, Wendy. I'm fine.

WENDY
Sit down and tell me what you've been doing all this time.

CHIG
There's not much—I'm very happy to see you.

WENDY
That's very kind, Chig.

CHIG
I'm—it's been a long time.

WENDY
Almost a year.

CHIG
Where have you been keeping yourself?

WENDY
In Africa.

CHIG
North Africa?

WENDY
No. Central Africa.

CHIG
That sounds like a nice trip.

WENDY
Yes, it was.

CHIG
I bet you got a lot of sun.

WENDY
It was wonderful. Noon for twelve hours each day. And you stayed in Europe?

CHIG
Yes. But I traveled around . . .

WENDY
I suppose you'll say you were tracking me down.

CHIG
In a way.

WENDY
Well, why don't you really tell me that?

CHIG
Excuse me?

WENDY
I asked you why you don't tell me you searched for me all over Europe? I might like that.

CHIG
Yes. Wendy. I was looking for you.

WENDY
Dear, Chig, you haven't found me yet.

CHIG
Why did you leave like that?

WENDY
Because you took too long.

CHIG
Excuse me? I mean, what did I take too long to do?

WENDY
How old are you, Chig?

CHIG
Twenty-nine. I'll be thirty next month.

WENDY
Why don't you get us some sherry. Please.

(CHIG briefly exits and returns with two glasses of sherry.)

WENDY
Look at me, Chig.

CHIG
Sure, Wendy.

WENDY
You're unlike any Colored I've ever met.

CHIG
Is that so? I can think of at least two others.

WENDY
Perhaps. But I believe you're perfect.

CHIG
Tell that to my mother.

WENDY
I'm sure she already knows.

CHIG
No. Everybody's disappointed in me. All for different reasons, though. Including me. I can't seem to get oriented. I've been . . . peripatetic for eight years now.

WENDY
But, Chig why?

CHIG

There doesn't seem to be a place for me; there . . . I don't know. Once I thought I'd be a lawyer.

WENDY

My father's a lawyer. He—but I won't talk about him. But I want to. I do like you, Chig. So until we get to New York, let's pretend we're not us.

CHIG

Excuse me?

WENDY

You should go to Africa someday, Chig.

CHIG

Would I like it?

WENDY

You'd love it. The girls are beautiful. They'd teach you important things about yourself.

CHIG

There are some Africans on this boat.

WENDY

There are? From where?

CHIG

The West Coast, probably. One said he spoke French, I think he said.

(Silence.)

WENDY
Are you really the person you seem, Chig? But if you weren't, would you tell me?

CHIG
Tell you I was—

WENDY
A big fat acorn.

CHIG
(Laughing.) A what?

WENDY
Haven't you seen any on the ship?

CHIG
All over the place.

WENDY
I know you have. But since you're on our side, it doesn't matter.

CHIG
It doesn't?

WENDY
No, dear-Chig. But please go on about those Africans.

CHIG
Well, there's not much more . . .

WENDY
Where did you see them?

CHIG
Down below. I was . . . There was a lifeboat drill and Wally—he stays in my room—and I were trying to find—

WENDY
What on earth were they doing down there?

CHIG
Well . . . I don't think we were supposed to be down there, but—

WENDY
Not you. The Africans. What were they doing down in the hold?

CHIG
They . . . they seemed to be . . . in chains.

WENDY
Chains. Chig, dear, don't you find that a bit unsettling?

CHIG
Well, yes. Of course.

WENDY
You said you spoke to one of them.

CHIG
Not exactly. I was talking to Wally and he spoke to me. He asked if I had the keys.

WENDY
How fascinating.

CHIG
It is strange.

WENDY
Why do you suppose there would be . . . how many?

CHIG
It was dark. If I had to guess I'd say near a hundred . . .

WENDY
Why do you suppose there would be a hundred Africans chained in the hold of this ship, Chig?

CHIG
Wally thinks they could be sailors who mutinied.

WENDY
But you think otherwise?

CHIG
It's just so . . . I don't know. I mean, I know Wally's answer makes sense. That would explain the chains. But if they mutinied, wouldn't the ship seem different? More unsettled? Anything happening up in first class?

(WENDY shakes her head.)

CHIG
You understand? The ship's normal, not like a hundred African sailors just tried to take it over. I admit, this is

only my second time on an Atlantic ship, but everything seems . . . normal. Besides, one African said he was coming for to be a slave. Something like that. At any rate, what do you suppose happened?

WENDY

The chains are the riddle, isn't that right?

CHIG

That's what I think. But . . . But I'm not sure he said it, because I'm a little worried about my hearing.

WENDY

Oh, Chig, that's not true.

CHIG

I don't know. People say things to me, and I don't understand them. Or what I hear doesn't make any sense.

WENDY

Do I make sense to you?

CHIG

You make perfect sense to me, Wendy.

WENDY

For goodness sakes, Chig, don't be so serious. You make me nervous.

CHIG

But, Wendy—

WENDY

Let me be very clear, Chig. I will never marry you.

CHIG

But why? Why can't you marry me? I mean, if you want to. You seem to like me. I don't want to get married on shipboard or anything.

WENDY

You're spoiling it. I just could never marry you. That's all.

CHIG

It's race. God, isn't that stupid.

WENDY

It isn't race. Race does not exist. If anything, it's culture. Don't think I'm stupid because my skin is white. It goes deeper than skin. I have relationships I shouldn't like to give up, places I go where you could not go. Race? It's ancest—

CHIG

But why don't we forget that and find out what we have as people?

WENDY

All right. But you still can't think you can marry me, Chig. Must I tell you everything? I'm not travelling alone. But until tomorrow afternoon, we can pretend.

(CHIG nods.)

WENDY
Now cheer up. Let me show you the real me, almost.

CHIG
Wendy—

WENDY
Are you ready for an adventure?

CHIG
I . . . what do you mean?

WENDY
Take me to the room.

CHIG
Well, I think Wally might be in there with—

WENDY
Take me to the room where the Africans are.

CHIG
Wendy . . .

WENDY
I want to see.

CHIG
I was hoping we could . . .

WENDY
We'll have time for other things later. Right now I want to see the Africans.

CHIG
I don't think we're supposed to be down there.

WENDY
Don't you want to solve the riddle?

CHIG
What if someone catches us?

WENDY
We'll say we're lost. We're looking for the infirmary.

CHIG
Wendy . . . ?

WENDY
It's better if we're not supposed to be there. It makes it dangerous.

CHIG
I—

WENDY
Exciting.

CHIG
Well . . .

WENDY
Please, Chig. Wouldn't it be a lark to sneak around? Like when you were twelve and you snuck out of the house to go to a high school party. We can pretend we're young

again. And everything's new and exciting. And everything between us is different.

CHIG

This is what you want to do?

WENDY

With you I do.

(Blackout. End of scene.)

SCENE EIGHT

(WENDY and CHIG are in the shabby corridor outside the slave room.)

CHIG
But what will we talk about?

WENDY
About why they're chained up.

CHIG
Why should they tell us?

WENDY
Why shouldn't they?

(They go to the door that WALLY had opened. It is now locked. WENDY puts her ear to the door.)

WENDY
I can't hear a thing.

CHIG

It's completely padded. I remember seeing that now. I think we should get out of here.

WENDY

But we haven't solved the riddle of the chains, Dr. Dunford. And I have reason to believe these waters are troubled.

CHIG

Now just suppose they really are, you know, slaves.

WENDY

We shall have to set them free, Dr. Dunford.

(Silence.)

CHIG

Well, let's hope Wally's right then.

WENDY

You're afraid.

(WENDY steps to the middle of the passageway and starts counting doors. She then begins trying to open one. It doesn't budge.)

CHIG

If they are slaves, the whole crew knows about it, which means that even if we did something, it wouldn't work.

WENDY

Don't be dreary, Chig. Besides, we haven't proved a thing yet.

(WENDY tries a second door. This one swings open into a small room with a desk and two captain's chairs.)

WENDY

Isn't this an enchanting little room! Come in and shut the door. We'll pretend it's ours.

CHIG

Let's not stay too long, all right?

(CHIG hesitates, then steps in and closes the door. WENDY begins looking over books and papers on the desk. CHIG joins her. He pats her shoulder lightly.)

CHIG

Don't touch anything, Wendy.

(WENDY picks up a number of various small books and examines them. CHIG finds a paperback that catches his eye. Eventually they find a stack of business-machine paper under a large paperweight. The sides of the paper are calibrated like film, a long list of words and numbers in columns on the paper. WENDY begins reading aloud.)

WENDY

SL2,220, 101/A22/GARDENER/6499.95
SL2,220, 102/A47/COOK/5999.00
SL2,220, 103/A34/SHOEMAKER/7399.99
SL2,220, 104/A33/BARBER/4990.00
SL2,220, 105/A42/POTTER/7444.95
SL2,220, 106/A29. . . . . . .

CHIG
Stop.

WENDY
What do you think now, my good doctor?

CHIG
That you should put that down and we should go—all right?

WENDY
Yes. But first we'll collect some evidence.

CHIG
There's plenty across the hall. Come on, Wendy.

(CHIG grabs WENDY's wrist. He takes the manifest from her and puts it on the table. Then he releases her. WENDY immediately picks it up again, tears out a page, folds it small and stuffs it into her purse.)

WENDY
All right, now.

CHIG
I guess we better just walk out, and if we run into anyone . . . pretend we're lost, like you said.

(OGLETHROPE arrives in the hallway.)

WENDY
All right, doctor.

(CHIG cautiously opens the door to the passageway just a crack. He sees OGLETHROPE standing in the hallway. CHIG takes a breath and they both step out into the hall.)

CHIG
Hello, sir. Which way is it to the infirmary?

OGLETHROPE
The infirmary, bud? Who's hurting?

WENDY
A woman's problem.

OGLETHROPE
I see. *(To CHIG.)* You're the one bunking with that, our boy Wally.

CHIG
Yes, I—

OGLETHROPE
(To WENDY.) I haven't met you, though. I'd remember that.

WENDY
My name is Wendy. Wendy Whitman.

OGLETHROPE
A prize to meet you, Miss Whitman. You got family in the mid-west?

CHIG

This is Mr. Oglethrope. *(Taking WENDY's elbow.)* Feeling all right, Miss Whitman?

WENDY

(Nodding.) I have family everywhere. We haven't all remained in Virginia.

OGLETHROPE

Virginia, huh? *(To CHIG.)* Maybe you don't need TYO after all.

CHIG

Do you know where the infirmary is, sir?

OGLETHROPE

To the end of the passage, make a right and climb the stairs. And take it slow for the little lady's sake.

CHIG

Thanks a lot, Mr. Oglethrope. Come on, Miss Whitman.

WENDY

I'm sure we'll meet again before this trip is over, Mr. Oglethrope.

(End of scene.)

SCENE NINE

(WENDY and CHIG are on the deck outside the lounge.)

WENDY
He's so muscular. Is your friend an athlete?

CHIG
I think so. I don't know him very well. What do we do now?

WENDY
About those Africans, you mean?

CHIG
Yes. The slaves.

WENDY
But, Chig-dear, they're not slaves.

CHIG
No?

WENDY
Certainly not. They're just plain Africans. It's an interesting idea, but . . .

CHIG
What about your evidence?

WENDY
What's wrong with you, Chig? I didn't say evidence. I said memento.

(Silence.)

CHIG
All right, they're just plain Africans.

(CHIG reaches for WENDY's hand.)

WENDY
Nigger? Don't you dare touch me! Unless I give you my expressed permission!

CHIG
I hope you and your friend have a pleasant voyage, Wendy.

WENDY
Don't pretend to be so God-awful polite.

(WENDY exits.)

CHIG
I'm not pretending. We house-niggers are bred to be polite. *(Pause. Then to himself.)* Wow.

(WALLY enters.)

WALLY

You're late for supper, Mr. Dunford.

CHIG

I'm a little overweight anyway, Wally.

WALLY

Huh?

CHIG

I'm only joking, Wally.

WALLY

Ya. Sure, Mr. Dunford, and they said you didn't have to sit at your assigned table on the last night, so I saved you a place.

CHIG

Thanks anyway, Wally. I'm not hungry.

WALLY

You have to eat, Mr. Dunford. You paid.

CHIG

You may be right, Wally. Let's go to dinner.

(WALLY and CHIG enter the lounge. LYNN and OGLETHROPE are waiting at the table.)

OGLETHROPE

I'm glad you came along, bud.

CHIG
So am I, Mr. Oglethrope. How are you, Lynn?

OGLETHROPE
You know Lynn, bud?

LYNN
Fine, thanks.

OGLETHROPE
Want some bread, bud?

CHIG
Yes, thanks. Did Mr. Oglethrope tell you he was looking for you, Wally?

(WALLY nods.)

OGLETHROPE
Found him too. Both of them. Going sneakers never pays.

CHIG
What kind of meat—

OGLETHROPE
Roast pig. *(OGLETHROPE does not seem to have moved his lips.)* Some nice-looking girl you picked up, bud.

CHIG
Isn't she, Mr. Oglethrope?

WALLY
He knew her from before. Right, Mr. Dunford?

CHIG
Just a second, Wally. Pardon me for asking, Mr. Oglethrope, can they talk? I mean, to each other?

OGLETHROPE
Let them try.

CHIG
I just wanted to know. So I wouldn't make a mistake.

OGLETHROPE
You're a cool one, Dunford.

CHIG
Am I?

OGLETHROPE
You think I don't know you were helping them go sneakers? You folks always meddle.

CHIG
Excuse me? Meddle in what, Mr. Oglethrope?

OGLETHROPE
In people's private lives. Can't really blame the kids. Not with folks like you around to ruin their outlook.

CHIG
Mr. Oglethrope, I don't understand what you're talking about.

OGLETHROPE
(With a butter knife in his hand.) You don't?

WALLY
It's all right, Mr. Dunford. He's right. I mean about me and Lynn.

(LYNN passes a note to CHIG under the table.)

CHIG
About what, Wally?

WALLY
He didn't help us, Mr. Oglethrope. We did it ourselves.

OGLETHROPE
Dunford knows everything, Wally.

LYNN
Please, Mr. Oglethrope. Please. Wally's sorry.

OGLETHROPE
Sit down, Lynn.

LYNN
Can I go now?

OGLETHROPE
By Tiwaz, sit down.

(LYNN steps away from the table. She rushes out.)

OGLETHROPE
If there's anything wrong with that girl, Dunford, I hold you responsible.

CHIG
Me?

OGLETHROPE
You, Dunford. Just watch yourself.

(CHIG nods, eats a bit more in silence and then rises.)

CHIG
I'll see you later, Wally.

OGLETHROPE
I've had him moved, Dunford.

CHIG
Good evening, Mr. Oglethrope.

(CHIG turns to exit. End of scene.)

SCENE TEN

(The cabin. CHIG enters the room reading the note out loud.)

CHIG

"PLEASE HELP MEET ME IN YOUR CABIN LYNN"

(CHIG looks up from the note and sees LYNN lying on the bed in a bra and panties.)

LYNN

Please help, Mr. Dunford.

CHIG

What do you want me to do, Lynn?

LYNN

Golly me, Mr. Dunford. Don't be silly.

CHIG

Now, don't you be silly. Whatever's bothering you, well, you'll forget it tomorrow when the ship docks.

LYNN
Think so, Mr. Dunford?

CHIG
I'm sure of it, Lynn.

LYNN
Don't you know what's bothering me, Mr. Dunford?

CHIG
Well, maybe I don't know exactly, but . . . but what I'm trying to say is that whatever it is that troubles you—understand?—it'll pass.

LYNN
Huh? Come on, Mr. Dunford, first touch me all over with your big black hands.

CHIG
Listen, Lynn, you don't really want to do this.

LYNN
You take a lot for granted, Mr. Dunford. Just because you're older than me doesn't mean you can tell me what I want to do.

CHIG
All right. I'm just trying to tell you that . . . sexual intercourse with me won't solve your problem, Lynn.

LYNN
Golly me, Mr. Dunford. Don't make me beg.

CHIG
Excuse me?

LYNN
It's not right. Every time I meet one of you fellows you always make me beg.

CHIG
Beg? One of who? For what?

LYNN
To golly me. Come on. I'm only fourteen years old.

CHIG
Fourteen years old?

LYNN
Did you read my file, Mr. Dunford? But my true age is seventeen years old.

CHIG
Lynn, wait a minute. Look. Why don't you get dressed, and if you want, we can go to the lounge—

LYNN
You can't golly me in the lounge. That would be real funny.

CHIG
But I'm not going to . . . golly you. *(Pause.)* All right?

LYNN
It's just not right! I know it's only an assignment, but it's not right for you to go out of your way to be mean. All the

TYettes said you fellows acted very nice about going golly, but every time I . . . Hey, Mr. Dunford, you're not Family Center-north, are you?

(CHIG shakes his head.)

LYNN

Some TYettes warned me about Family Center-north, said they'd kidnap you, but they said the Family West-northwest talked tough, and demanded respect, but could get real sweet, and you know, and that Family Center fellows like to go golly when they weren't working, because everybody knows business comes first with the Family. Though Mary-Joan Dinley even lived with a Family Center agent when she was assigned to the Cameroons. Until the authorities found out. But she went too far, having a baby and all. But I'm assigned to you so take off your clothes.

(CHIG begins unbuttoning his shirt, realizes he still wears a coat, takes that off, and resumes with the buttons. Then he stops abruptly.)

CHIG

You're making a mistake, Lynn.

LYNN

You must be new, Mr. Dunford. Didn't any Family tell you about the TYettes?

CHIG

I don't think so.

LYNN

They should've. I was fourteen when Daddy signed me up, and I don't remember doing anything at all. But after Basic, I was just like everybody. Hurry up, Mr. Dunford. Wally'll come in fifteen minutes.

CHIG

Fifteen minutes?

LYNN

I go very fast.

CHIG

Where's Wally now?

LYNN

Over in the office with Mr. Oglethrope. We might even have time for two.

CHIG

With the slaves?

LYNN

With the cargo. Ya. You recording, Mr. Dunford?

CHIG

No, Lynn.

LYNN

Because Mr. Oglethrope goes real berserk if I get recorded. You and Whitman really have him flumixed. We were told it was only her, and maybe a backstop. Now he doesn't know how many . . . Please hurry, Mr. Dunford.

CHIG
Listen, Lynn, wait here a minute.

LYNN
Where're you going?

CHIG
I have to go to the infirmary.

LYNN
Don't worry, Mr. Dunford. After Mary-Joan, the authorities called us back for adjustments. Honest, Mr. Dunford, in three years both on the north and south Atlantic run—

CHIG
I'll be right back.

(CHIG steps out the door. LYNN pulls a pistol out from under the pillow and goes to the door looking after CHIG. End of scene.)

SCENE ELEVEN

(WALLY and OGLETHROPE are in the office from SCENE EIGHT. CHIG sneaks down the passage outside and eavesdrops from outside the door.)

WALLY
You're all wet, Mr. Oglethrope.

OGLETHROPE
I've been at this longer than you, kid.

WALLY
I'm telling you, if we do it your way, it'll jam. The TYO480 won't accept it. Honest, Mr. Oglethrope, this is something new.

OGLETHROPE
Back off, Wally. I've done these things since the war, and I know how to make them short and brief. You think I'm not acquainted with the agent who reviews our work? We know how we operate; we got an understanding.

WALLY

This is a new procedure. They don't want just plain cancels. They want us to report in detail.

OGLETHROPE

That's the stupidest thing I ever heard, Wally. We fill in the blanks and go back to work.

WALLY

Well, all right, Mr. Oglethrope. I can't dispute my superior, but I think it's only fair to say I'm planning to submit my own report.

OGLETHROPE

You got your channels, and I got mine. But don't take credit for my cancel.

WALLY

Whatever you say, Mr. Oglethrope.

OGLETHROPE

Hmph.

(WALLY begins to whistle. CHIG crosses the hallway to the room where the slave was seen before. As he is turning the knob LYNN creeps up behind him. She has put on a pair of pleated pants and a TIWAZ YOUTH ORGANIZATION T-shirt.)

LYNN

Ready for some exercise, Mr. Dunford?

CHIG
You have a key?

LYNN
Sure, Mr. Dunford.

(LYNN produces a key and unlocks the door. She opens it to reveal the room is now pink and filled with exercise equipment—a punching bag, a medicine ball, exercise horse, etc. LYNN urges CHIG into the room and closes the door behind them. CHIG stands transfixed, taking in the complete removal of any evidence of the slaves that were here.)

LYNN
We have to talk fast, Mr. Dunford. Were you kidding in the cabin?

(CHIG nods.)

LYNN
Yes? *(Pause.)* Don't be mean now, Mr. Dunford. I'm real sorry you lost this game, Mr. Dunford. Did you know her well?

(LYNN produces a pencil from her pocket and goes to a pad of paper hanging on a chain near the parallel bars.)

LYNN
I would never get a feeling for Wally. If he got cancelled, I'd be sad.

CHIG
Wh . . . Whitman's cancelled?

LYNN

Sure, Mr. Dunford. So I'm giving you my address in New York in case you change your mind.

(LYNN tears off a piece of paper and sprawls on the floor to write.)

LYNN

Were you in love, Mr. Dunford?

CHIG

Yes.

LYNN

That's nice. Maybe I'll fall in love one day, but never inside TYO. And Family fellows are out of the question. They showed us movies of Mary-Joan Dinley.

CHIG

She lived with an African?

LYNN

I guess so. He was Family Center. You're Family Westnorthwest, aren't you?

(CHIG nods.)

LYNN

What Family was she, Mr. Dunford?

(LYNN finishes writing and jumps up to bring him the paper.)

LYNN

I told Mr. Olgethrope she was Family Center-north, but—

CHIG

Wendy's Family? Wow. She was passing!

LYNN

You mean you didn't know either? This was really some game. It's the most interesting since I joined.

(OGLETHROPE enters from the office.)

OGLETHROPE

So you lost this game, Dunford. Next go maybe you'll get the breaks. But not against this TYO Team. For a while, your offensive had me fooled. I was looking at another colored girl. A ginger-cake. Where'd Whitman say she was from?

CHIG

Hmm. *(More softly, to himself.)* "Don't you dare touch me, nigger."

OGLETHROPE

What's that, bud?

CHIG

Virginia. Family Westnorthwest.

CHIG

(To LYNN.) Are you finished with that, Lynn?

(LYNN looks at OGLETHROPE and crumples the paper in her hand.)

LYNN

Finished, Mr. Dunford. Maybe next time.

OGLETHROPE

Right! This game is over. Dunford, I know you're new in the game, and maybe it'll surprise you that through the years some customs, you might call them, have grown up between TYO and you boys. You might wonder why we didn't cancel you. Simple. We transferred the cargo, so why spill oil we don't have to? *(Pause.)* Anyway, after we take the prize we usually offer you boys a beer, you know, and we all toast the cancelled. So I'm hoping you'll join us.

CHIG

Thank you, Mr. Oglethrope, but not tonight. I couldn't possibly. *(Pause.)* No.

OGLETHROPE

Just a second, bud. I don't think I understand. You act like you believe I didn't like her. But I did. I watched her offensive, and at the end, of course, we took the prize. Yes, sir, boy!

CHIG

(Checking his watch.) No thanks. I want to get some sleep. This was my first game.

OGLETHROPE

Sure, Dunford. *(To LYNN.)* You see how these boys play for keeps? That's the way you have to be if you want to expect to win.

LYNN

But, Mr. Oglethrope, you assigned me to go—

CHIG

Good night, everybody.

OGLETHROPE

I assigned you as a mousetrap move, Lynn. But you got to vary your offensive. You don't golly every time you get assigned a target—

(CHIG exits. End of scene.)

SCENE TWELVE

(In the lounge LYNN is seated, dressed for the ship's arrival. CHIG enters in a daze.)

CHIG

Hello, Lynn.

LYNN

Mr. Dunford? I tried to get down to your cabin last night, but . . .

CHIG

I understand. But, Lynn? *(Pause.)* Where do you stay in New York?

LYNN

Golly, Mr. Dunford, I'm sure glad! Can you remember? In Westchester, you know the area code, Richland 850—

(HARRIET enters wearing brown-rimmed glasses like cat's eyes.)

HARRIET

I hope I can sit down, sugar, because this Harriet is surely pooped.

CHIG

Sure, Harriet did you say? Have a seat.

HARRIET

(Seating herself.) Thanks. You been aboard this whole trip and I didn't see you?

CHIG

Lynn, this is Harriet.

LYNN

Hi, Harriet.

HARRIET

How long you been in Europe, dear?

LYNN

Huh? . . . Well, like my Mom says, three's a crowd, Mr. Dunford. And I have to find Wally. He's my boyfriend, Harriet. Bye-bye, Mr. Dunford.

CHIG

I'll call you, Lynn.

(LYNN exits.)

HARRIET

Now that she's gone, sugar, tell me your name too.

CHIG
Charles.

HARRIET
(Nodding hello.) Charles.

CHIG
Most people call me Chig.

HARRIET
Charles . . . Chig. Charles, I could never begin to tell you how tired this sister is. Nothing but travel for a whole month. The first week I was on a tour, but then I didn't go with them people anymore, just walked around looking. I bought some beautiful shoes in Rome, thinking they'd be nice for my job, but sugar, I walked those shoes to death. What did you do?

CHIG
I travelled around.

HARRIET
I'm a writer. *(Pause.)* I mean I cover society news and human interest for The Citizen. It's Harlem's only daily newspaper.

CHIG
I remember seeing it.

HARRIET
You lived in Harlem?

CHIG
All my life until I left. Over between Convent and Amsterdam. My folks still live there. I still have to pack.

(CHIG stands and heads to his room. HARRIET follows.)

HARRIET
I hope you don't mind my coming with you, sugar. I'll help. We all need a little help every now and then.

CHIG
Well—

HARRIET
You know, I bet if we'd met sooner we'd be close friends by now. Since we didn't, this will be the perfect way to start.

CHIG
I suppose that would be all right.

HARRIET
I didn't even know there were rooms over here. I guess on a boat this big you sort of find your own spots and stick with 'em.

CHIG
I guess so . . . You know, that girl, Lynn, that I was talking to . . . you'd never guess what she was into . . .

HARRIET
Honey, let's not talk about that girl now. Oh hey, I bought the finest bottle of European brandy, wanna taste, sugar?

CHIG
Hmm?

HARRIET
I really planned to save it for my editor, but hey, he probably wouldn't know the difference anyway. *(As they enter the room.)* Here, have a taste.

CHIG
Thanks.

(CHIG tries to grab his bag, but HARRIET takes it from him.)

HARRIET
You just sit down and relax and let me take care of this.

CHIG
You don't have to—

HARRIET
I'm an excellent packer. I used to be the world's worst. I could never get everything in there. Then I learned to roll my clothes.

CHIG
Roll?

HARRIET
Now I love to see how much stuff I can get into a suitcase. You know? I can't wait to get home. I've been cravin' a good ol'fashion burger, grits, sweet potato, somethin' . . . that food they've got over there in Europe, whew, sure

makes me appreciate America that much more. Don't get me wrong. Europe is absolutely amazing. Beautiful. The art. The architecture. And those Italians really do know how to cook. They've got this one dish, Penne all' Arrabbiata—it means "angry pasta"—that is so spicy it'll knock your socks right off your feet. But sometimes a body's just gotta have chicken and waffles. A few things surprised me a little when I went over there. I thought I'd be livin' it up, but boy . . . those hotels . . . the things you take for granted. You have to walk down the hall just to go to the bathroom, oh excuse me, the water closet . . . and the toilet paper . . . that stuff was so rough I thought I'd surely scrape my behind right off, or as they say, my bum. But, I mean, like I said. It wasn't all bad. I don't really have a burning desire to go back to France, but could certainly watch a few more Roman sunsets. Well, I do believe I've got everything packed away here.

CHIG

Amazing.

HARRIET

Oh, there wasn't that much to pack.

CHIG

It was still amazing. *(Pause.)* I think we docked a few minutes ago.

HARRIET

Well I suppose we ought to be heading off.

CHIG

Thanks for all the help. It's been . . . a pleasure meeting you.

HARRIET

Sugar, just because we didn't get on this boat together doesn't mean we can't walk off it that way.

(HARRIET takes CHIG by the arm and begins leading him down the ramp.)

CHIG

I...

HARRIET

You headin' to Harlem?

CHIG

Well, yes. My family lives there.

HARRIET

Great. I'll share your cab.

CHIG

Well. Ok. I don't see why not.

HARRIET

Just let me get my things together, here. It'll just be a minute.

(HARRIET disappears into her "room." Her voice is recorded for rest of paragraph.)

HARRIET

I'll go back there someday. To Rome. I have to—I threw my three coins in the fountain. One to accomplish your dreams. Two to find your soulmate. And three to come back to Rome. What a beautiful wish—coming home. When you leave you can't wait to get where you're going. But when you set sail for home it always feels like you can't possibly get there soon enough. *(Stepping back into view.)* You ever feel that way, Charles?

(They continue down the ramp.)

CHIG

Yes. I suppose I do.

HARRIET

Hey, I know just the place to take you to.

(CHIG and HARRIET walk the rest of the way down the ramp and are in the bar.)

HARRIET

I think the taxi driver thought we travelled together, Charles.

CHIG

That's all right.

HARRIET

What's the matter, sugar? You're shaking.

CHIG

Yes. I know.

HARRIET

Charles, what's the trouble? Oh goodness, what's his other name? Chig?

(CHIG sits up, still shaking.)

CHIG

I'm tired. I'm just tired, man, am I tired.

HARRIET

Just relax, because this music will give you the thrill of your life. This bar is owned by none other than the Golden One himself, Jack O'Gee. Anybody might happen to come in. All kinds of distinguished ladies and gentlemen, congressmen, beauty-parlor queens, number-runners, judges, musicians, movie stars, preachers, visiting taxi-fleet owners from Chattanooga, the manager of the ex-fly-weight-champion of the world, Skeeter Jimson, I met one night, Cripple Christopher on his wooden leg, Shorty Moreland the midget m.c., and just about any other bodies you could think of.

(Throughout the bar scene voices of people at the bar are heard amplified.[1] *CHIG and HARRIET go to a table against the wall with a long bench seat.)*

(Pauses.)

You see this place always has a good conversation going on. Just listen to that. It's its own kind a music. *(In response to the voices.)* Hondo's one of the fastest-mouthed cousins I ever heard. Every time I see him, he has a new story.

(Pauses.)

I really should try and talk with him. Charles, you'll have to forgive me, sugar, but I want to do a little work.

CHIG

Yes. All right.

HARRIET

You sure you don't mind?

(CHIG sits back and relaxes in the safety of Harlem.)

CHIG

Na. Human interest for The Citizen. Go on, Harriet. I'll wait for you. No one's expecting me. I can stay out as long as I want.

(BLACKOUT.)

End of Play

[1]The voices heard throughout the bar scene may say part or all of the following text:

"... Am my body had been in at that time, if he ever try to pull some knife on me, man, and you buy the next do it whenever I get to drinking, I also get to thinking about we, Marky Electo, and Julius Chambernard, his brother Roger, and Norton Williams standing in that same bar bell or something, a bus-stop sign with a stone bottom on her Paul and Terry picked that mother over his head with one hand and pressed it five or ten times a day I be getting up and running to the bathroom last winter some or other time, I recall, staying home and the snow start falling by the window. Now I never been exactly what you'd call a Polar-bear, you understand, but that snow sure looked seven kinds of good to me. Because of what me and my man've just go through. Right, Juan?"

"—trying to tell you something about the time I sold my soul to the damn Devil; then tool that soul right straight back again. . . . Not that I ever got convinced by his Devil stuff, even after he made me sign my name in blood. The man had some money for me. But Juan, he started to carry garlic around in his pocket!"

"And we got some money. Devil had me put on this dog collar beat out of gold and covered with precious stones, and then, went away and forgot I was wearing it. We sold it to what they call a private collector for, now let me tell you, twenty—time . . ."

NOVEMBER
1977

time twelve years later, finding him the professor tenured settled and teaching. "How come you never got married, Professor Dunford?" Dale Hoenir's question surprised him. In their weekly conferences, they usually discussed literature and closely related subjects, almost never anything so personal as marriage. The very topic of marriage, let alone any personal ramifications of it, came as such a surprise to the professor that a trickle of coffee caught in his windpipe, causing him to gag momentarily and his eyes to tear.

He quickly recovered, dared to answer honestly. "The only two girls I ever wanted to marry, well, one didn't like me and the other didn't love me. The second one I knew around the time I first met your cousin."

"You mean Uncle John? Did he know her?"

"He may have. I didn't know everybody she did." Wanted: one Wendy Whitman, dead or alive, hopefully, but impossibly, the latter. "Come to think of it, I didn't know her very well myself."

"But you loved her." Her intonation made it a statement.

The professor nodded, keeping the word "Yes" to himself.

It still hurt, more than a decade later. "But does all this have anything to do with Huck Finn?"

"Not really. And not with any other supposedly great American novel. Can you think of any great American books about marriage, Professor Dunford?"

"About marriage? Not offhand. But come, Dale, let's get down—"

"Don't get professorly with me, Professor Dunford, Uncle John already told me you're a softy. But . . . I'm thinking about getting . . . about marriage and how little there is about it in what everybody considers the great American books. Just look at *The Scarlet Letter*. Honestly! And where's there anything about marriage in *Moby-Dick*. Or *Gatsby*. Think about Daisy and Tom! Not even *Gone with the Wind* has much to say about it, good anyway. Our most creative minds ignore it. No wonder nobody knows how to make it work."

"Oh my parents do. They've been married almost fifty years." The professor hoped he did not seem to brag about his parents, but he did love and admire them.

"Yes. Mine do too. But nobody quote important unquote writes about it, except as something noble but in a state of ruins like Foro Romano. Were you disappointed in that pile of rubble, Professor Dunford? I was." Suddenly, she stretched, and the professor became aware of her height, an inch shy of six feet. She had written about her height in an autobiographical poem she had shown him, calling it her "bittersweet blessing." She wrote good poetry, desperately in need of pruning, but the real stuff there early.

"Dale, I think we're getting way off the point here. What about your *Heart of Darkness* essay?"

"As a matter of fact, Professor Dunford, I wrote it this morning. I just haven't typed it up. I'm having personal difficulties. At least I consider them difficulties."

He waited, dreaded the coming earful. Hearing confession pretty much came with a faculty position at a little college like this, but the professor, a man fat and shy, never knew what to do with the information received. Life had taught him that the path had many bumps for all. Nod your head sympathetically and counsel patience, he thought. Everything always takes too long to happen.

"I think I'm getting married. In June maybe. And it's ruining my plans because I didn't want to get married at least til I had a Master's, which is four years."

"You feel you'll have to leave school?"

"I can't see any way out of it."

"Anybody I'd know?"

She shook her head. "You might know of him. He plays baseball. He's got a baseball scholarship." Sitting up straight and prim, she added, "Honestly, Professor Dunford, I promise to get caught up before the year ends."

They conversed about literature then, Dale Hoenir's personal difficulties disappearing behind conjectures concerning *Gatsby*'s Daisy and Tom. Finally the hour ended.

Dale donned her bulky spring jacket, gave her shoulder-length hair a quick comb, and strode out into the March afternoon. From his office window the professor watched her crossing the cozy campus quad, headed, he realized in amusement, not for her room or the library where one might type an overdue paper, but toward the college's thawing soggy playing fields.

In April, the professor got a second glimpse into the personal life of Dale Hoenir, coming oddly enough on the day she unloaded all her overdue work onto his office desk, announcing: "Looks like I'll be here next year, Professor Dunford. I broke up with my baseball player."

The professor treated the subject as lightly as the girl

seemed to. "I'm glad to see you caught up, Dale, but I hope it didn't cost you a love life."

"It didn't." She smiled, sadness haunting the edges of it. "I don't think I'm really destined to get married, at least not til I'm as old as you are."

"Youth can be so cruel to age," he said quietly. "But do you really believe in destiny?"

She gave the question serious consideration. "Oh just say I know myself pretty well, though for a minute there I doubted it. I have a lot I want to do, Professor Dunford, poetry I want to write and books to read. I knew I couldn't really settle down and cook for some egotistical baseball player. Some people can spend their whole lives dreaming of making big money!"

Lack of understanding and a grave nod linked together more and more as his years crept by. How much less he understood now than back in the sixties. How much more foolish he habitually felt. No wonder Wendy Whitman had not loved him. "You found your ballplayer a mercenary sort?"

"Sure, isn't everybody? But you can't allow yourself to overestimate the value of the skill you're selling. You have to be reasonable even when you're dreaming!" She seemed momentarily annoyed with herself. "Anyway, you're disinvited to my wedding, Professor Dunford. Funny, the sand castles you can build on the head of a pin," she went on. "I could see myself baking bread and cakes every day, cooking good things to keep up his strength, and teaching at the school local to whatever team he played for. Then in a few years he'd make the Big Leagues and I could go to the games, raise kids, and write poetry. Could've worked, don't you think?"

"I guess it depends on the scheduling. I've heard the life of a minor league baseball player is no bed of roses."

"Sure, Professor Dunford, I didn't have any illusions about that. He wouldn't make much money and he'd be out of town half the summer. But I could write when he went away, or like I said, teach school. And a baseball player's wife must see some interesting things. I could keep a diary. But—"

The professor had stopped listening, Dale's sketch of the smalltown life of a minor leaguer's wife taking root and blossoming in his mind. Scene: A neat little apartment in a neat little house in a neat little town. Birds chirping at the kitchen window. Dale Hoenir at the kitchen table, typing poetry. Faceless athlete enters in uniform with baseball bat over his shoulder. Old-fashioned glove hanging from the bat. Dale and faceless athlete bend to kiss . . .

"But he doesn't play baseball that well. Good enough for Double-A, maybe, but really, Professor Dunford, he'll never make the Big Leagues!"

Exit faceless athlete. "How can you know that, Dale?"

"Because I know baseball; I'm a baseball fanatic. I'm a Bronx girl, born and bred in the only borough of New York City on the mainland of America. I went to public school and Evander Childs on Gun Hill Road. My grandpa Hans had practically a farm on Bronxwood Avenue at East 229th with chickens and goats. He grew carrots and tomatoes. He had a white grape arbor and made rhine wine in his cellar. He died only ten years ago, so I was big enough to remember him. He loved baseball. And if you love baseball, living in the Bronx compares to living in heaven. Because the Bronx has the Bombers, the best. Grandpa Hans took me to my first baseball game at the Stadium when I was about three. He used to tell me he waited til I got out of diapers because he didn't want to bother changing me in a last-of-the-ninth-two-out-two-on-two-behind situation. Sometimes Dad or Uncle John would go with us, but mostly it was Grandpa Hans and me. So over the years I've seen a lot of baseball, the best mostly." She paused, took a deep breath, studied her knuckles, sighed.

"He'll never make the Big Leagues. The air up there's too rare for him. He's a step too slow in the field. His arm is only so-so and he can't hit a curveball. Honestly, Professor Dunford, how could I ever marry him not really believing in him? He loves playing the game so much. And how could I tell him I don't believe in him and still marry him?"

The professor shifted uneasily in his armchair. He had no answer for her, and so avoided her questioning blue eyes. All the same he admired her integrity. Or perhaps she had displayed not integrity, he thought after she had gone, but an instinct for self-preservation. Why tie oneself to a man who bid fair to fail? Why sign on to witness that failure? Much better to let him live his failure in peace without the additional responsibility of a wife and children. As for Dale, she clearly had better things to do with her life, an academic career to build, poetry to write. Or so the professor thought.

But Dale Hoenir had other ideas. Within a month she and her ballplayer had left school, disappearing into the South somewhere. The following September the college registrar mentioned to the professor that Dale Hoenir had requested the forwarding of her transcript to a college near Columbus, Ohio. The professor heard nothing from Mrs. Dale H. Jurgensen herself until the following February, winter's grayest month, when her letter found its way into his mailbox in the Faculty Room. He made note of the Florida postmark on the hotel envelope. Quietly excited, he returned to his office, slit open the letter, and read:

Dear Professor Dunford,

You should see my tan, and we only arrived here four days ago. The hotel has a pool shaped like a baseball glove and right now, writing you, I'm sitting near the pinky. What a year we've had! I thought to write you before this, but we did a lot of moving around, from New York to Tennessee (where Viking hit .434 with 29 homers and a local sportswriter gave him his nickname) and then to Ohio where we took the fall term, then Christmas in Louisiana with Viking's dear sweet parents and then in Florida for Spring training.

We expect to spend the summer in Ohio (Triple-A farm for the Bombers) and after that, who knows? Things look good for Viking's chances to get called up toward the end of the season. The top brass paid for our whole trip here because he's such a good prospect. Remember I told you he couldn't hit a curveball? Well, you learn something every day. It doesn't matter about the breaking pitches because they have people who can teach him to hit them. The important thing—he can hit a fastball! Any fastball, even the fastest notch on the batting machine, about 120 miles an hour, and that's 20 miles an hour faster than most humans can throw. He has phenomenal vision. I sure underestimated Viking's ability. Maybe I just dwelled too much on what he couldn't do. Nobody seems to care about his slow running (five seconds from home to first base) or his poor arm. They're too busy trying to get him out, which they can't. He walked over one hundred times in Tennessee, and struck out only twenty.

Maybe you'd like to know how we got back together. I remember leaving your office one day feeling awful, but at the same time you'd got me talking about

Grandpa Hans who always told me to go to the top. So I did. I wrote a letter to the Boss of the Bombers and told him all about Viking, how much he wanted to play and how we wanted to know if he could make the Big 5 and that our whole lives practically depended on the answer. And guess what? He wrote back. Even though the season had already started, he said if we could get to Tennessee, Viking could get a tryout. Maybe he thought we wouldn't take the chance. So I used some money I had saved and we rode a Hound to Tennessee. I figured it was worth it to find out, for both of us.

Anyway, we got to Tennessee and nobody could get him out. He hit in his first fifteen straight games. Somewhere along the way, we got married. That's just the way it happened. But here comes Viking. We have to go to the ballpark for a uniform fitting and a photo session. Bye for now. Thanks again.

Sincerely,
Dale

P.S. In Nashville I started writing song lyrics. Sold a few. It's fun.

The professor put the letter aside and leaned deeper into his chair. He did not follow sports and so understood only the bare bones of her narrative, the business about breaking pitches and poor arms mystifying him. He could tell only that the girl had taken a chance with her Viking, that the chance had paid off, that she seemed happy. And why not? Perhaps he dwelled too long on what he could not do and did not have. Perhaps one day he might even get married. Who could tell? Just when you seemed to have it all sorted and tied and filed away into dull green cases, up jumped life, bringing not always disaster, but from time to time . . .

DECEMBER
1985

time of the darkest night of the darkest week of the darkest month of the darkest season of the darkest year of the darkest decade, professor Charles Dunford stood at sunset near the plate glass window of the observation lounge at Vermont International Airport, wiped the steamed glass with his hand and tried to pick out his niece from among the debarking windswept passengers. He could not have missed her. Along the line of bundled and laden travelers, she strode serenely sockless in sandals, flimsy cotton skirt and tube top under an open wind-whipped man's dress shirt. She had shaved the entire left side of her coppercolored head bald and plaited the reddish kinky right side into many tiny braids and affixed each braid with a jadegreen bead. She appeared to have at least two perhaps three holes in each earlobe and earrings in each; a gold stud glittered in her left nostril. No hat. No gloves. Charles Dunford went to the arrival lounge.

His niece had traveled with one midsized magenta nylon bag and carried it, so Dunford hurried her through the terminal and out to his car. As they waited for the motor to warm and heater to function, he noticed that she had got so cold that no steam came out of her body with her breathing.

"Did you forget your coat somewhere, Merry?" He half-meant the question. She did not seem stupid, just thoughtful and detached. "Or maybe it was summer when you left Boston."

"Cold doesn't bother me, Uncle Chig." A smile fluttered on her lips, a sign she meant no hostility. "Never has."

"Obviously! But I feel cold just looking at you." Though she did not look at all cold. She looked quite comfortable. Actually, as the warmed air blew throughout the compartment, she began to dew, a bead or two on her upper lip. "Did you even bring a coat?"

"I have a heavy sweater in my bag." She gave the magenta nylon two pats. "For really cold days. Can we stop talking about the weather please?"

"Sure thing, Merry." Dunford shifted into drive and steered the car out of the parking lot, pausing to pay, then onto the highway back to Capitol, inwardly grumbling. On the third of December he had received a letter from his sister Connie, who lived with her husband in Washington, D.C. His sister had enclosed an instant-foto of her youngest child and only daughter, Merry. He compared the foto to others he had received over the years and marveled at the quick passage of time. One day an ugly baby and the next day an outlandish creature almost grown. Same eyes same nose same mouth but all the rest of the baby face stretched to adult size.

Dunford's sister had asked him to let Merry stay with him for the spring term and attend the high school in Capitol. For two and a half years she had gone to a prep school in New England, but refused to return in the spring. And Connie did not want her finishing high school in D.C. So until she could make other arrangements, could Merry please, please finish her junior year in Capitol? Besides it would give Dunford a chance to get to know his niece. It all seemed harmless, but the instant-foto told him that Merry looked like trouble. All the externals might seem merely comically exotic had not her young eyes transmitted the profound disenchantment and pugnacious defiance of the archetypical teenaged rebel. Dunford had seen the expression a few times in the eyes of his own students. He recognized it and wanted none of it.

That evening he phoned his sister. Okay Connie tell me what's really going on with this kid. Connie's voice had a sly edge to it. It's like she fell to earth from a distant planet. Which one? Just from the instant-foto you sent I'd say Mars, almost human but not quite. Connie had laughed sardonically. I was awake at her birth, so I know she's mine. But don't rule out some kind of alien life form. You're not serious, are you? He wondered if his sister had started to lose it. She had always held up pretty well in stressful situations before this. Perhaps she had started to wear out, had sprung a leaking hole in her soul. Underneath it all, she's still sweet, his sister had continued. Like a flower, she was always a sweet baby . . .

Dunford remembered his niece as a quiet watchful baby in a playpen. One summer afternoon in 1968 he had visited Connie and Clive when they still lived in Philadelphia, Dunford and his brother-in-law sitting in the small backyard of the small house in a small mews south of South Street, where Clive (who had Caribbean roots) grew his own cabbage, callaloo, cannabis, and cucumbers. Connie came and went from the kitchen, where she had a lasagna baking. Baby Merry Fairchild sat watching from her playpen. She never fussed or cried. She sat in the center of her playpen and watched the two grown men getting stoned and making fools of themselves . . .

Now Merry sat beside him. Against his better judgment, he had agreed to let her stay the spring. His sister had always known how to get him to do things for her. He had always wanted to please her, and heard the gratitude in her voice as Connie and he made their goodbyes.

They crossed the ice-glutted Winooski River into Capitol's Main Street and pulled into the lot of the Capitol Market. "I have to do some shopping. Can I get you something you like, a favorite?"

"Just some fresh vegetables. And fruit. Lots of fruit. Any kind. I don't eat any meat. Or cheese. Chicken and fish sometimes."

He did not shift his attention from his parking, but seemed to hear some contradictions commencing already. "No trouble. I'll get some iceberg lettuce. You like lettuce?"

"Romaine please." She inhaled sharply through her nose. "Do you resent me staying with you?"

"Resent you?" He bought time, forming an answer. " 'Resent's' not the right word. I don't know what to make of you. But I don't have any reason to resent you. Yet."

"Well, did you want to bother with me this spring?"

He decided not to lie. "I wasn't crazy about the idea. Nothing personal. When I wasn't teaching, I'd planned to spend the spring finishing my book on Dupukshamin."

Timber! came the far cry of the distant . . .

"I won't stop you." Her voice stayed flat. "I spend lots of time reading."

"Then I guess we'll have a quiet good time of it." He shifted into park. "Anything else besides romaine? Tomatoes?"

She did not answer.

Without looking at her, Dunford got out of the car, leaving the motor and heater running, entered the supermarket, and picked up a plastic basket. Strange kid, he thought, not as hostile as her image, more like bemused, seeking the ultimate Cosmic Answer. He had seen dozens of them. Just a kid really. He wondered if she had become sexually active, then marked how his thoughts always returned to contemplation of sex, figuring it into every life equation. See a pretty woman with nice breasts and a bunch of grapes in her hand and imagine her holding your brown bat and balls instead. Fruit. The kid wants fruit. He halted in front of the altars of banked oranges and grapefruit.

"Now I have a teenaged vegetarian on my hands," he said to the woman holding the grapes. For two years he had seen her around the college but did not know how she connected to it. "Wants fruit. Vegetables. No meat. Some fish."

The woman looked up from her purple grapes. "What did you say, Professor Dunford?" She startled him, knowing his title and name.

"I have a teenaged vegetar—"

"Vegetarian," the woman interrupted. "I did hear you. That's easy. Get her some figs. You should have a teenaged survivalist to shop for. They eat bugs and worms."

"Salted, or unsalted," he came back quickly, sensing the woman's desire for verbal intercourse. "As antipasto or main course?"

"Fried with garlic butter, my dear." She flipped her wrist in graceful imitation of aristocracy. "See, my son went to a survivalist camp last summer. The first day his counselor marched them out into the forest, had them dig up a worm and eat it. Yum." She made a face. "To break down their squeamishness right away. Yum. I said to my mom, I'm paying so much money so he can eat worms and bugs all summer?"

"Now he's developed a taste for worms." Dunford jumped

ahead to the point. "Well, I guess that's not much worse than escargot. I wonder how many people would eat them if the menu just said snails."

"Yum . . ." She made a face, drifting away with her purple grapes, then shouting over her shoulder. "Don't forget to get her some figs, Professor Dunford!"

Disoriented by her familiarity, Dunford turned to the fruit and vegetables. He selected a bag of carrots, checking that it held no rotten ones, then romaine lettuce and three bulging tomatoes, more succulent than the packaged ones. So far so good. He would relate to the kid in her own terms, but, as a gesture of welcome, give her some sophistication.

Since the Capitol Market catered to students and faculty from all over the world, as well as politicians from all over the state, it got in a wider variety of produce than most towns in Vermont usually offered. With the guidance of friends, he had sampled much of it. He picked a soft black avocado and a bright mango like a smooth calico cat and some ripe bananas, which all his life he had liked with milk, sugar and flaked corn. He put a bunch of kale in his basket, noticing the colors, realizing how drab his habitual food palette had become over the years. He tried new things, but ended up eating the same old things. He chose some yellow squash, enjoying its shape, wondering how to cook it. At the Shaddy Bend School they'd served it mashed—ugh—and his mother never cooked it. But he could read, he reminded himself, and had several good cookbooks on his shelf. Thinking of the grape woman and her nice breasts, he took up two wheels of figs, the dark plump kind, and tossed them into his basket, then headed for the checkout counters.

Ahead of him waited the grape woman, grapes now bagged in sheer plastic. "Did you find what you wanted, Professor Dunford?"

He shrugged his face. "I don't know. I'll just have to want what I found." He rested his basket on the corner of the counter. The cashier finished packing a large purchase.

"Such an interesting way to put it." The grape woman had two long black braids, bound at bottom by thin strips of white leather. "Do you study eastern religions?"

He wondered if anyone had ever introduced them. "Not in any organized way. I dabble."

"But you captured the essence." She spoke to him so intimately he felt sure they had met before, but could not conjure up a place of meeting, a cocktail party or faculty tea. "Wanting what comes your way."

"Next please!" the midlife matronly cashier called. "How're you doing tonight, Miss Bravo?"

"Not too bad, Mrs. Plembley," the grape woman said. Bravo, Dunford thought. Funny, she didn't look Hispanic to him. But neither did that actor with the Irish face who'd changed his name from Rodriguez. Over the years, Dunford realized, he'd seen or met many individuals who did not look like their names sounded. *Timber! came the far cry of the distant woodsman* . . . For example, the titan Alexao Dupukshamin, the study of whose life and works had occupied Dunford for decades. Nothing he'd read in English-language monographs prepared him for the luxuriant black ringlets which framed the author's swarthy face, or the broadness of his nose or the fullness of his lips. Clearly an Aesop lurked in the fuel supply of Dupukshamin's aristocratic ancestry. In the U.S. there existed not one image of the author that Dunford could find. In his infrequent angry moments, he even entertained the idea that a conspiracy of scholars deliberately kept from the English-speaking world that one of the great novelists of nineteenth-century European literature came of sub-Saharan stock. They had revealed Pushkin and Dumas, but drew the line at Dupukshamin. Let him stay white like Shakespeare or Beethoven or Alexander Hamilton or Warren Harding or Mae West or J. Edgar Hoover, whom R. A. Hodges had exposed as descendants of Africans . . .

Meantime, as he stood pondering all this, Miss Bravo (wherever they'd met, if ever) had completed her business and left the store. Mrs. Plembley had taken the opportunity of Dunford's reverie to light a cigarette. "You ready now, Professor?" She chuckled. "You college types're a kick in the butt! Get an idea and freeze like a deer caught in your headlights. If I stopped punching my register every time I got a good idea, they'd fire me sure."

"No, they wouldn't, Mrs. Plembley." He emptied his basket onto the conveyor belt and she began calculating his purchases. "Because you're married to the manager."

"Knowing Plembley, I'm not so sure." The cigarette bobbed between her thin lips in a round face. "You know what I mean, Professor. I saw you talking to Miss Bravo. She's a strange one."

"Why?"

Mrs. Plembley blinked, looked blank. "Well, what about those braids? When'd you last see a grown woman with her hair in braids?" The matronly cashier had her hair done in a style that even Dunford, who hardly knew the difference between a bustle and a miniskirt, recognized as a hairstyle that held sway in the nineteenforties, tightly rolled bob and pompadour. "That's sure strange I'd say."

Dunford wondered how Mrs. Plembley would feel about the hairstyle presently occupying his automobile, wondered what she'd say when she did see it. "I don't know about that. Braids're kind of universal and timeless. I mean, everybody from Navajo to Austrians—"

"That's fifteenfortyfive, Professor. But you're talking about foreigners." As he reached for his money, she began to bag his groceries. "Austrians. I mean, they live on the other side of the world, by gosh, and upside down!"

He ignored the faulty geography. "But Navajos aren't foreign."

"Look, Professor, we're all native born, but our descendants all came from somewhere else!"

Drop it, his soul said to him, drop it. She has a mind like quicksand. The more you struggle. But he gave it one more try. "I still don't think braids're such a strange way to wear your hair."

"My hair?" She pushed his bag of groceries toward him, took his twenty, worked the register. "I never wore my hair in braids in my life! Too strange for me!" She gave him his change.

He pocketed the change and picked up his bag. "But as I've often said, Mrs. Plembley, I consider you an extraordinary woman." He smiled. Flash dem whites.

"O Professor, you sure do have the gift of gab." He read confusion in her eyes. Good, the old bitch. "Merry Christmas!"

"Have a nice day, Mrs. Plembley." Even though the wall-clock read sevenfortyfive. He backed away from the counter toward the door. "And Happy New Year."

Free in the cold air, he looked down the main street of Capitol where he'd lived the last ten of his fifty years, when everybody else went home for holidays or vacations, the only spook for miles. Joking that if he ever moved away, the Africamerican presence would disappear from that frigid corner of the universe. Talk about white, the snow stayed white for a week after it fell, never turned to slush, melted and trickled away clean enough to drink. Down Main Street, the City Fathers had strung arches of Christmas lights, old-fashioned and perfunctory as a condolence card to a distant cousin. Cars packed with already drunken teenagers cruised beneath these arches as carols struggled with the bluster of their souped-up motors. The store windows socked it, for Vermont at least, strings of extra lights, a few new displays. At thirty dollars a tree, Dunford hadn't gotten one, hoped Merry wouldn't miss it.

The car stood as cold as a tomb; Merry had turned off the motor, but looked crisp and fresh as watercress in chipped ice.

"Hope I didn't take too long."

"It gave me a chance to get my head together." She seemed to have matured four years since he left. "I mean, I ain't had such a hot term."

The "ain't" surprised him. "Rough?" He put the groceries on the back seat, then climbed behind the wheel. "And what about that 'ain't'?" the grammarian in him couldn't resist asking.

"Don't worry, Uncle Chig, I get A's in English. And everything else. But life."

Starting and warming the motor, he glanced her way to see how seriously she took herself, found her sitting at attention sniffing the air.

"Did you get figs? How did you know to get figs?" She rose, twisted climbing to her knees, leaning over the back of the front seat and diving into the groceries. She returned with a wheel of figs, tearing into the cellophane wrapping. "I dream about figs, Uncle Chig, actually dream about them."

Dunford navigated the car out of its diagonal slot and into Main Street traffic. Instead of heading home up Barry Street, he decided to keep straight on Main to show the kid the town. At the State Street stoplight a carload of smashed teens came alongside, peered, marveled at Merry's big-city hairstyle, silently jeered, then roared away past Bob & Jolly's Original Ole Time Ice Cream Parlor when the light blinked green.

Concurrently, Merry devoured her fifth fig, chewing vigorously mouth closed, a lady, sighing closemouthed with pleasure. "Moooom."

Her sudden mood swings threw him off. "They have good things there," he said to fill the silence.

At the corner of Langhorne Street, he slowed to point out one of Capitol's popular bookstores. Hunched over the book-laden table just inside the door, like a chimp in a glass booth, Dunford recognized the hairy face of his fellow teacher and boss, chairman of the Comparative Literature Department, Professor Raymond Winograd. Almost eight, the store had emptied and Mrs. Reade had got up from the cash register near the door and toddled back into the rows of tables and bookshelves to give them a closing-time straightening, leaving Raymond Winograd alone near the front, unaware that somebody saw him thieve two paperback books into his black parka's voluminous pocket, then give his puffed pocket a pat. Through the layers of glass that separated them, Dunford watched Raymond Winograd silently mouthing a casual goodbye to the unseen Mrs. Reade, pull open the door, step into the street, take and exhale a steamy breath.

Dunford sped off quickly, hearing the sound of his niece chomping into her tenth fig. Bemused, he repeated: "They have good things."

"These are the Turkish kind, I think, the chewy grainy sweet kind. So far these are my favorites." Merry leaned back and relaxed down into her seat beside him. In the streetlamp's light her bald head glowed like an egg lit from within, fringed with the kinky reddish braids on the other side of her head, her shellshaped ears studded with gold. Though kind of freckly, almost mariney, Merry possessed one of the classical African profiles, the cute nose one that often ages cute but can also turn bloated and bug-eyed depending on its possessor's self-discipline, like Shirley Spackleton, the first girl he'd ever kissed on the mouth. Built up to it for weeks. Fantasized about it for two months, since the summer night her folks (devout Bayjans) had actually let her come out for an hour after supper. In August 1947. Just twelve at Greenwood Lake that summer. On her screened porch that ran around the house, the pines scratching the screens when breezes blew. Spackleton had that funny accent. Me na call yu Chig it sound like disease mon me call yu Charles like yu fatha. Shirley had black hot comb bangs, cute. Cute little figure too, even later in college. After Avis, he took her out a few times but the heartpounding love stilled. Puppy love the strongest love for Shirley and Chig. A very nice girl, but Avis had ruined him for Shirley. Saw her at a teachers' convention still looked good married forever.

"You know what I dream about figs? I'm walking on an empty beach with purplecolored sand. And the sky's a kind of lilac, a pastel purple. And the sun's a vibrant rust really hot because in my dream I'm barefoot and have to strut across the sand, but after while I get used to it or I forget about it. And Pop's there with Youngbro too, but not Mom or Bigbro. I don't miss her. I mean she's somewhere around, but not with us just then. So we're walking on this beach under the broiling rustcolored sun, but not sweating. And we forgot to bring lunch so we get hungry. Then Pop calls us over, and we gather around him and he holds out his hands with the palms up. Then figs start to grow out of the ruts in his hands, like little balloons blowing up, and we pluck them off and eat them. They're so pungent and sweet I can't describe how good they taste. I love figs, even growing out of my Pop's hands!" Merry crumpled the cellophane from the figs into a ball. "I hope you weren't waiting til we got to your house to eat some figs, Uncle Chig, because, guess what?" She opened the window to a blast of winter to dispose of the cellophane, thought better of it, closed the window retaining the trash in her fist. Nice girl.

"Glad you liked them. I got those for you. And there's another package in there. A woman in the supermarket suggested them."

"Must be a special lady," Merry commented.

They had continued north turning east on Main Street, passing the doctor's house and the Main Street School, and just before they reached the Vermont Culinary Institute, took the right turn into College Street, beginning the climb up to College Campus, which sat like a fortress on top of the hill overlooking Capitol and the Winooski River and more roundtop hills beyond the river. Dunford wondered how Miss Bravo had known figs would prove such a sensation. He wondered if he'd actually seen Raymond Winograd shoplift two paperback books. Patpatting pocket proudly.

"What do you think my dream means?"

"I'm an uncle, not an analyst, my dear," he answered crisply. "But Dupukshamin has a similar dream in one of his stories, *The Hermit*. The hero—"

Timber! came the far . . .

"Who?" She sat straight and turned toward him.

They crested the hill, two blocks ahead saw the lights of College Church belltower. Took two books. Crook. Always so concerned about the integrity of the department. Crook.

"Dupukshamin, you mean? Alexao Dupukshamin."

"Never heard of him."

"What about *The Red Cavalier*?"

"Oh, that was like *The Three Musketeers*. I ate books like that about four or five years ago. When my breasts first came in I'd hide in my room and read books by the armload. Can't remember who wrote any of them."

"Well, Dupukshamin lived at the same time as Dumas and

Pushkin, and they all had roots in Africa." Dunford heard the teacher tone enter his voice. "He was born in 1800 . . ."

She did not respond. They had reached his home on Nelson Street from the top end, passing the College instead of climbing up from Barry Street. Turning right into his short driveway, he had to look at her, finding her suddenly immersed perhaps in her dream. He pulled into the garage and switched off the motor, then closed the garage door behind them, shutting out the cold.

"This is it, kid."

"Kids are goats." She opened her door. "That's what Mom says."

"That's what my mom says too."

"She got that from Grandma?" She gathered up her magenta bag and swung her legs away from him and thrust her feet out the far door. "I guess that sounds like Grandma. She's—"

Dunford hefted his tummy and fat butt out of his door, stood up, and shut it. "You were saying?" He opened the rear door, but perceived that the grocery bag rested closer to her side. He closed the door.

"Actually I stopped because I don't want to say anything negative about your mother—"

"Your grandma. You were going to say that it was the kind of thing a person would say who also says, A place for everything and everything in its place, but then doesn't follow her own axiom."

"And don't count your chickens before they hatch."

"Does Connie say that too?"

"At least once a day, for each."

They burst out laughing. When she stopped, Merry opened the rear door on her side, bent over and picked up the bag of groceries. Arms full, she bumped the door closed with her hip. Dunford rushed around the car to take the bag from her, but she shook her head, chin raised. "You have to unlock the door."

He chuckled. "We don't lock our garage doors in Vermont."

"In 1985?" She raised her eyebrows. Foto didn't show she had them, made her look weird. Just faint baby hair. Flash foto faded eyebrows faint. "They wouldn't let us have locks on our doors at school and two girls got raped."

He resisted the urge to leap on this information and make a big thing of it, instead held open for her the door connecting garage with kitchen, reached inside and snapped on the lights. Merry stepped into his home. "Just put it on the counter." He noticed his phone machine blinking red. "And I'll show you your room. When I travel, I always like to see where I'm sleeping when I get to a new place."

Merry stood in the center of the restored nineteenth-century woodpaneled kitchen, swiveling slowly on the flat heels of her sandals. Her toes looked healthy, smooth and walnut brown, like they'd just come in from a warm summer afternoon. Even through furlined boots, his feet froze.

"This room really speaks to me, Uncle Chig, the wood." She continued turning, her eyes glowing in the kitchen's soft light, a rosetinted bulb off shining wood. "Mom's kitchen is all white plastic and chrome, like a kitchen in a hospital." She paused over what she'd said. "I'm not too tough on her, am I?"

"Your mom has a right to her little compulsions, Merry."

"I like the way you put things, Uncle." She didn't add his name. Somehow it seemed more not less friendly. "Show me my cell and straw mat."

"It's a little more comfortable than that, I hope." He guided her past his livingroom and up the stairs to the second floor, which had three small bedrooms and one large bathroom, her bedroom nearest the stairs, separated from his by the bathroom and the middle bedroom, which he used as a storeroom for books and things he'd outgrown or which had painful memories attached to them, though he also had an attic. He only went into the middle bedroom when he had to unload some part of his past, a book associated with a failed romance or articles on Dupukshamin he could not place in scholarly journals even after many submissions, finding a place for each and all on his shelves, then retreating with all deliberate speed. But he kept the first bedroom as dainty and quaint as an old greeting card, with a creme bedspread crocheted by his father's mother, Nanny Eva Dunford, on the four-poster the old lady had actually slept and died in, though he rarely told that to any guest. On the wall above the headboard hung a portrait of her, darkbrown and wrinkled, white kinky hair like a halo, fierce-eyed. Dunford had commissioned an artist to paint it from fotos he'd taken of her on a trip to the South he'd made in 1952 with his father, one of the few times he'd met her. On the front porch, legs crossed at the ankle, hands knit in her lap. Now sit up straight, Nanny, he'd mustered the courage to pose her. Don't slump. She obeyed, after resistance, eventually sensing the importance to him of the occasion. Captured her spirit with the old Argoflex.

"That's your greatgrandmother, Eva. I don't think she was ever a slave. She used to say she came from Africa and arrived as a baby in 1866. But I don't think she was born til at least 1872."

"She looks like she would've given slavery a hard time." Merry sat on the edge of the bed, testing the springs, bouncing. "Pretty firm."

"I'll go downstairs and fix a little supper." He backed out of the room, pulling the door behind him, walked down the hall to his own room. Without turning on the light, he emptied his pants pockets onto the bureau, an evening habit, then retraced his steps, passing her closed door, downstairs to the kitchen. There he removed his camel-tan parka and furlined shoes, donned his mashedback moccasins, feeling his feet relax. Dunford wiggled his toes into warmth.

Again, his phone machine blinking caught his eye. Wondering who'd call. Three days til Christmas. Perhaps Connie and Clive phoning to check if Merry arrived safe and sound. Or some sad news waiting in the machine. In the old days if somebody called with sad news and caught a person travelling, sad news couldn't wait there in the machine for him to come back. Sad news would have to call again. But why assume sad news? He laughed softly at his pessimism, rewound the messages.

"Hello, Charles. Raymond Winograd calling. We have an emergency here to address, Charles. Concerning the integrity of the department. So if you get in before eleven give us a call so we can straighten it out. I'm really quite concerned and when the matter came to my attention I was really distressed. So even though I know we're on vacation I doubt you'll mind coming by my office. I'll be in all morn—" Saved by the beep, Dunford thought. Raymond Winograd wouldn't call back to continue his message. Too cheap. He'd think over what he said and decide that he'd said enough. Crook. Right there to see him do it. Destiny. Wow.

The machine had continued, changing voice: "Professor Dunford? This is Renka Bravo phoning because I forgot to say to you that we're having an open house party on Christmas afternoon if you and your teenaged vegetarian feel like getting out of the house. Plenty of figs and avocados, which figlovers seem to like too. I meant to tell you when I saw you but it skipped my mind so if you can come, please call me tomorrow at International House. Byebye."

The machine beeped and continued: "Professor Dunford,

Suzu phoning." The department secretary. "Mr. Winograd just phoned to say you'd be dropping by the office tomorrow and well I think he wanted me to remind you that we haven't received your share of what we agreed to give the Winograds to celebrate their seventh wedding anniversary. We bought them a VCR. He told me he really needs a second one. He . . . hinted he expected a Christmas gift too. See you tomorrow. Bye." Suzu always made a clatter hanging up, like she never quite hit the cradle on the first try. Probably looking at something else on her desk. Working late. Department couldn't run without Suzu. Winograd didn't know sparrow doody about . . . damn fraud.

He turned to the sink and began to wash his hands, using a drop of dish detergent, then wet the dishrag and wrung it out, wiped his hands. He wondered if Winograd wanted anything else from him besides his contribution to the Winograd Semi-annual Appliance Fund. Does that a couple times a year. Last time, Lilith's birthday needed fifteen toward a new PC. So here comes Suzu doing his begging. Did you know Mr. Winograd's dog's birthday's this Thursday? Yes Suzu but I wanted to forget it. Shhh. I think he's in there. Suzu taking it as a joke. "Crook," he said aloud, sighed. "Now what do I want to cook for this kid?"

First of all he'd prepare a big salad. A salad couldn't miss. He unpacked the groceries he'd bought, having difficulty finding space on his stocked shelves for his purchases. Fat and getting fatter, even shelves getting fat. Enough is enough and too much spoils, Benjamin Franklin said. Arabs too. Fat man himself. Franklin. In his youth people described Dunford as chunky. Chunky Chig become chubby Charles. No matter what he did to stop the process. So a salad might. He stopped himself from hoping what it would feel like to get back in shape again. Really.

"Stick to the salad." He arranged lettuce and tomato and celery and carrots and onions and garlic on the counter in front of him, a menu forming in his mind. Something very simple. He halffilled the sink with cold water and dumped all the vegetables into the water, giving them a quick rub and rinse, then let the water out of the sink and left everything to drain while he filled a gallon pot with water to boil spaghetti.

With wooden matches, he lit the burner, adjusted the flame. A few years earlier he'd decided against a new electric stove, preferring gas flame over anything but natural untreated charcoal, remembering the country people of Reupeo shoveling ochre earth on top of a blazing woodpile, making a smoke-seeping mound, days later digging into the mound for logs of burnt wood which they smashed into smaller chunks with an axe. Timber! Charcoal. The third trip to Reupeo he'd cooked on charcoal or wood and considered himself an expert at lighting a fire with one match and one sheet of newspaper and six twigs of kindling. Substitute dry grass for newspaper. Give him that and he could burn down the world. Burn baby burn.

"Please, Professor Dunford, such violent imagery." But he'd come to enjoy bringing light and warmth out of one match. Of course it had taken more than one match for him to learn his lessons about fire. Average American can't light a fire or keep it lit. Lighting fires in the windy Reupeon evening. He'd lost some pounds the first few months he spent in the country researching the early life of Dupukshamin. Wonderful weightless days. Consuming piles of newspaper and wasting matches. Chopping his vegetables all jagged and ugly. Stomach growling waiting for the water to boil. The same soup night after night til Saora Capeurtao taught him to make fry bread. Laraonsa made fry bread light like crepe. He'd have to make some fry bread for Merry. She might appreciate the adventure of it. Americans, especially those who hadn't travelled, hate fry bread. Take a few chews and make a puzzled face. Too tough for teeth accustomed to cherry danish. Left unfinished. Wasteful. Reupeons devoured mounds of fry bread. Fry bread and OldNinety. Well-fueled work all day. Maybe she'll like it. But not tonight. "Tonight it's *spaogetto ol dontao* with garlic fried in olive oil."

He began peeling vegetables. Nanny Eva Dunford that first trip downsouth in fiftytwo had taught him to peel vegetables. Respect the food, Charles. That God food. It passes through you in about two days. If you use it right. Asking about did he have a movement today. He knew if he'd stayed longer on that first visit to grandmother that she'd have forced some black sulphurous laxative into him. But they didn't know each other quite that well. And he'd just turned seventeen and she wouldn't mess with his manhood forcing him. As she'd taught him the dampened onion and garlic skins came off easier wet than dry. Wash everything first. Fierce-eyed. Exacting. No wonder Pop ran away and became a doctor. Fierce-eyed.

He scraped his sharp kitchen knife down the outside of the carrots, rasping off the bitter part, the raw pulp glowing more orange, thinking about those first two weeks downsouth. Couldn't believe the craziness of the segregated drinking water fountain. A pipe coming out of a wall and way over there through six feet of pipe, the COLORED fountain. Moronic! Absurd! Yet people died. Funny how one image. Not the shame, the absurdity. What kind of mind could come up? If they really had the courage of their convictions they'd have just forbade us to drink water away from home and finished the debate once and for all. But separate but equal? To go to the expense of an extra fountain, what a joke? Still there it stood and we took a snapshot of it and didn't have the courage to drink from the WHITE fountain. Though nobody stood guard. Didn't feel bad about it, more puzzled. Felt lower than cowdung when they wouldn't let us eat at Woolworth's. Where we spent lots of time and money upnorth. Good burger deluxe on Saturday after the movie with the guys from Shaddy Bend. But couldn't get a deluxe downsouth. Didn't even know if they had it. Still hurt anyway. A woman actually telling us, we don't serve colored here, not just a sign on the wall. Pop looked weak objecting sputtering. Butbut. Butbut. Pop wanting waffles with butter. Butting his head against a stone wall. Summer 1952. Could've had sharpshooters with rifles ready waiting to plug any niggers who sipped WHITE water. The whole thing absurd. A sickness. A bankrupt idea. No scientific basis for it. Most blacks mixed up with whites anyway. We're both; they're one. So who's better? We're all; they're a part. What're they afraid of would jump from our lips to the spigot and wait for some unsuspecting cracker and turn him what? What did they fear? That they'd catch nigger from the water fountain? He snorted a laugh. "All about money anyway, not race. Someone was selling more pipe. Someone was getting paid to put it in."

Dunford wished he'd had some emeraldgreen raw spinach to add to his salad, it would look good with the orange carrot chips he chopped. Oh well tomorrow after Winograd's office we can. And figs two more packs. But maybe not take Merry to Winograd's. The way she looks might so peculiar. Half and Half. All those earrings. Watch it, sound like Mrs. Plembley about Miss Bravo's braids. Renka Bravo. Could be a stage name. Vaguely remember she dances.

On the bias he sliced crescents of celery, added them to the carrots in the oiled wood bowl. The two tomatoes he cut into eight wedges each. Then he tore the lettuce into dollar-sized strips. "Don't cut lettuce, Charles, cutting wilts lettuce." He tried to imitate Nanny Eva's voice, the age and authority he remembered from a third of a century before. In his head he could hear her voice clearly, but he couldn't make his voice sound the same way. He made a salad dressing of mustard and olive oil and vinegar. Nanny Eva's voice had vinegar in it. Fierce-eyed.

Finally he chopped the garlic and carefully heated two tablespoons of olive oil in his small skillet. Watch this now: Might burn the garlic if oil too hot. He dropped chopped garlic into hot oil and watched it sizzle, bubbling tiny bubbles white against the black pan, then at the edges, turn brown. Watch it! Burn no garlic here tonight! In from the edges garlic burned tan. He turned off the flame.

As the garlic cooled, he started the spaghetti, dropped a halfpound pack, like pickup sticks, into boiling salted oiled water and spread it around the pot, poking it with a wooden spoon til it started to wilt and submerge. He covered the pot and turned down the flame a bit, considering it a little defeat if a pot boiled over. Sssss.

Dunford sat down at the kitchen table and knit his fingers, releasing his spirit into the quiet. He had always enjoyed sitting alone in kitchens, especially clean and cozy kitchens, even Mrs. Dale's arrangement of ranges in the basement room, more lab than kitchen, at the Shaddy Bend Upper School seventh-grade cooking class. Mrs. Dale taught it as precisely as a scientist, all measurements and oven thermometer and timers. Learned from her though. Funny the teachers we remember. Laughed behind her back at her prissy ways, but loved the cooking. Got a B-plus, deserved A-minus. Didn't give A's. Just can't get by on natural ability, Chig. Should've asked, why not? But her scientific approach counterbalanced Mom despite best intentions a chaos in the kitchen, all dither and piles of dirty utensils to boil an egg. Didn't know Mom's Mom. Died before. Northern creoles catholic. Never raised to cook. Pretty bemused lightskin in those few fotos. The formal portrait—Vandercamp, 1926—with the faraway gaze. Like what happened to our creole world, the picnics and cotillions, in her eyes. Ssss.

The spaghetti boiled over, hissing. He leapt to the stove and lifted the lid releasing some steam, a billow. Out of the boiling frothy water, he fished a strand of spaghetti, finding it crunchy at the core. He sat back down. Two more minutes to *ol dontao*. Sounds like the name of a town in the Reupeon Hills. Two minutes to ol Dontao, my sir. Old train chugging along, coming to a stop in an ornate station. Chunky brown-skin stranger debarking. Close-up of sign saying "ol Dontao." Wonder if that spaghetti's.

He checked the pot again, finding the spaghetti tumbling, all stiffness steamed away. He set a steel colander in the sink, then, using potholders to grasp the hot handles, poured the water through it, catching the cooked spaghetti. He rinsed off the starch with running water and let it drain, before returning the spaghetti still steaming to the pot. Then he spooned the browned garlic and oil onto the spaghetti and mixed it around, careful not to break or tear any strands with his fork and cooking spoon. Everything all ready to serve. Kid should like. Not too heavy. Nine o'clock. Not too late.

Quickly he set the table, place mats, forks and soup spoons for twirling, glasses, then went to the foot of the stairs and called her name. In a few seconds, he called again, and started climbing to her room. "Merry?" he called through the closed door. He knocked. "Merry?" He opened the door. "I'm coming in, Merry."

She lay asleep, peaceful under the glowering protective image of her greatgrandmother, on her right side on the still-made bed, her hands pressed together against her pressed knees and drawn up toward her chest, as though she might finally feel the cold reaching into the room from the winter night. But the room felt comfortable to him, the new furnace installed the winter before doing its job. Who can account for the changes of teenagers? he thought, stepping to the closet for a light wool blanket, which he grasped by the corners, and spread over her. She didn't stir, but in the ashtray on the bedside table fluttered feathery ashes.

"Wait a minute." Dunford circled the bed, closing in on the ashtray, finding four spent matches, a quantity of white ash and one half of a thin handrolled cigarette of cannabis sativa. Now he smelled the dead smoke in the air, like chestnuts roasting on an open fire or those punk sticks we used to burn on summer nights. Or church incense. He went to the window and let in a blast of winter, scattering ashes to the four corners of the room. Still Merry slept, blanketcovered, secure. He closed the window to a crack of cold air.

In the ashtray only the spent matches and halfjoint remained. Now what to do with that? Down the toilet. But does she have more? He picked up the ashtray and its contents and turned toward the door. A concerned teacher now, he decided to save the evidence til the morning and use it as a pretext to lecture his niece on the rules of the house. Just as he pulled the door behind him, she stirred slightly. "Thanks Uncle," he thought he heard her mumble, but never knew for sure. He closed the door.

Save it til the clear light of morning, he thought, descending the stairs with the ashtray held next to his heart. Save it for the clean crisp light. After a good night's rest and now don't make me into a policeman, of course in the old days we all smoked this stuff but the difference we didn't start til our twenties but these kids at seventeen and younger. Can't do your system any good. Smoked some with Clive back in the sixties. Wonder if he still? Could secretly. In Reupeo we smoked haosh or keurf. From Africa. Smuggled across the Mediterranean into southern Reupeo. Got it up in Smepriroa's only African restaurant, Lao Colaonbein. Could never find out what that meant. Lao Colaonbein. Menu had a strange flower on the cover but not a soul knew. Chicken with peanut gravy better than we imagined. Eating that white stuff like dough (fufu?) with our bare hands dipping into the dish with everybody else. *He that dippeth in the dish with me.* Getting full. Then some primao would light up a big fat spleurf right there in Lao Colaonbein. Showing no fear of cops and their white staves. A next and another lighting up. Til the joints got jumping. Joints and spleurfs going around. Took a quick puff and passed it. Afraid. But the Reupeons stuck with OldNinety. Illegal brew too, but theirs. Big penalty if the Authority caught a Reupeon smoking a spleurf. Trace the evil all the way back to the Crusades. Castration or something. Sultan Kutyakokauf. Deep dark dungeon. Decades disappeared. Done.

Downstairs, he put the ashtray and contents on the kitchen table and decided to force himself to sample his cooking, fears about Merry smothering his appetite, feeling bad for his sister, knowing how upset she must feel to have her daughter experimenting with drugs. Well, smoking cannabis anyway. Dunford had stopped considering cannabis a drug after he started smoking it himself. Nice at the beginning. Then didn't have any for several years. Then at Lao Colaonbein. With fork and spoon he piled spaghetti studded with toasted garlic into a bowl. "None since seventyfive. Ten years. Wow."

Dunford hadn't liked some of the screwball ideas smoking cannabis gave him. Especially when he smoked it alone. As long as he could smoke with a nice bunch of people, like in Europe those years and from time to time in some congenial setting and some cannabis coming out and going around and everybody stayed friendly and nobody got offended or paranoid and everybody got a little high and laughed at silly stuff and had a good time. But not since seventyfive. With that guy Bedlow in a car outside the Golden Grouse. Back in Harlem.

He took his seat at the table, whispered a thankyou, then sprinkled the spaghetti with grated cheese. Using a spoon as a backstop he wrapped strands round his fork, took a mouthful and chewed. Not bad. Not bad really. Kids probably shouldn't til oh maybe eighteen. Same with cigarettes or beer. Got drunk on beer a quart that summer at camp. Fifteen. First time. Head spinning staggering through the woods to make a piss. Funny getting drunk the first time but never so good afterwards headaches next day. Just something to do at a party, to make the boring seem witty with white wine. Cannabis had never given Dunford a headache. Just a dry throat. Wanted to drink water. Cola. Orange juice. Cranberry. He swallowed. "I should have something to drink with this. Cranberry juice. Good for that bladder problem."

Dunford stood up and stepped to his fridge, took out the magenta juice and poured himself a cup into a coffee mug. Glasses made him nervous. He always feared he'd break them, especially the longstem kind. He preferred even the most expensive beverage in something unbreakable and steady like a coffee mug. He sat back down to his plate.

"Hope she doesn't do anything worse. A little smoke never hurt anybody. With emphasis on the little." But Dunford knew he had to give his niece the standard AntiDrugLecture. He took another mouthful of spaghetti and chewed, mulling it over. Can't get any around here. But wait of course she can. Between the politicians and the college kids. He sipped his juice and swallowed all. Really needed a kid with a drug problem coming into the house about now. Really needed that. Just got rid of a truckload of problems for a few weeks. Now Connie unloads this one in my lap. "Could always get me to do—"

The front door chimes singsonged. Dunford wiped his

mouth with his napkin, getting up. On the other side of the livingroom by the front door he stopped to check his face in the hall mirror, brushing several grains of grated cheese from the corner of his mouth. Looked at his watch. Ten. He opened the door, realizing too late he had not checked.

"Professor Dunford? I hope you won't think I rang too late but I saw your lights on and I took the chance you wouldn't think I'm completely nuts to stop and invite you again and your niece because we'll have lots of nice kids there too at our open house on Christmas afternoon."

"Miss Bravo?" Wind flapped her long rustcolored coat open to something purple.

"Please. Renka." She had a nice smile, corners up, perfect teeth.

"Renka." Should I? Why not? "Do you want to come inside? I just broke open a fresh magnum of cranberry juice."

"If it doesn't . . ."

He shook his head. "Come in out of the cold for a minute." He opened the door wider and she stepped in, leaving an intoxicating scent the same as the African woman, probably Senegalese, he had passed on rue Raspail in Paris that time spring sixtyeight. A little like Joy but darker. Nice breasts too. "You want to take off your coat?"

She had not stopped in the livingroom, but had gone on through to the kitchen. Dunford marveled at her temerity, then shrugged and closed the door. Entering the kitchen, he found her sitting at the table, wiggling out of her great rust coat and draping it over her chair's back, staring at the half-consumed cannabis cigarette in the ashtray, and beyond it, at his plate of spaghetti.

"So glad you smoke hemp. It makes all the difference—"

"But wait—" Royal purple dress trimmed with gold, pigtails wrapped with white leather. Nice breasts.

"—if a person smokes a little hemp. I tried coke in the sixties, never did it again. Made me want to kill my husband, and I liked him. Never dropped any acid. Hate, I mean, hate needles. I once dieted on speed. Believe me it burns you up. And pills? I don't even take cold medicine. I rely on herbs, hemp and a little red wine sometimes. What about you? How do you dull the cosmic pain?"

"The cosmic pain?"

"Well actually clarify the sources of pain." She smiled, her mouth not smiling much, but her hazel eyes smiling almost constantly. "Everybody's doing something to alter this or that mood. Do you really know anybody who doesn't take anything but food and water? Even my granny takes a little nip."

"Pretty cynical." He stepped closer to the table. "You really believe that?"

Her words did not go with her looks. Renka Bravo talked like a bigcity smartmouth, but she looked more exotic, like Miranda Audobon or Chiquita Maureeno or the raven haired oliveskinned English actress Siobhan Maugham, who all his parents' westindian friends swore up and down had passed from Bayjan to Rhodesian on the trip from Arawaka to England. Renka Bravo could have passed, Dunford mulled, but from what to what? Hispanic to Navajo? Brazilian? Jewish? All kinds. Not a race. Lightskinned Africamerican for Mexican maybe?

Meanwhile, she continued chatting. ". . . why I don't let but a few people know what I'm doing, let them think what they want because if you let an artist onto a college campus, you should know better than to expect her to transform herself into an academic type since you started out saying you wanted artists on campus to bring some Diversity." She opened a deep purse, rummaged in it. "Well, honey, color me Diversity!"

Dunford sat down across from her. "You are so colored."

"Must have some African in there somewhere." She looked up at him. "Oh you mean Diversity. Do you mind if I drop your first name, Professor, and just call you Dunford?"

"Sure." He eyed his plate, wished he could stop talking and eat. "But I wanted to explain about the cannabis—"

"Don't vex yourself, Dunford. If your supplies get low during the winter, I always have some. I keeps me some smoke." She chuckled cheerfully, and resumed rummaging.

"But I wasn't smoking when you came in," he insisted, determined to set the record straight.

"Of course you weren't." She sniffed the air, setterlike. "You were eating. Garlic? And I interrupted you. I'm sorry." She sounded sincere.

Surprising himself, he heard his voice say: "I made enough for two, but my niece fell asleep. Can I interest you in some?"

Again she paused in her rummaging. "What time is it?" She pulled her hand out of her bag bringing a metal film canister. "I have some more at home. I can give you what I have here."

Dunford shifted uneasily, answering her question. "About tenfifteen." He didn't look at his watch, remembering he had checked the time when she first rang his chimes. "You don't have to—"

"Hemp I share, Dunford. What is that, *spaogetto eurlao e al jao*?" Her good Reupeonese impressed him. "Let's just smoke the rest of yours while you warm up the pasta." She put the film canister on the table, placed the halfjoint between her lips, plumbed the depths of her purse again, coming up with a transparent yellow lighter. "Unless you want me to do it."

"You don't know my kitchen." Dunford stood up and lit a low flame under the spaghetti pot, wondering if he should warm his plate, but how.

She lit the end of the thin cigarette, inhaled smoke, held

it. Her face relaxed, lost all expression. She held her breath for a minute, her face growing nearly beautiful in its stillness, an oval face with hazel eyes, brown now in the mellow kitchen light. She exhaled. "And holding your breath helps to calm you down." She held out the cannabis to him.

Dunford sat down again. "I haven't smoked any of this in a while."

"Until just before I came." Her eyes smiled shyly, warmly.

Dunford began again to protest his non-use, then paused realizing he would then have to explain who had started the cannabis smoking, a betrayal of his niece. He shrugged, took the heat. "Til, just before, I found some I hid and forgot."

"I do that sometimes. Especially if the bag was good and I didn't want to smoke it up too quick."

Dunford chuckled, resigned, took up her lighter, lit the cannabis and slowly inhaled, feeling the smoke catch in his throat, stifling a cough, holding his breath, heart pounding.

"Lots of dudes don't bother to hold the smoke in anymore, figuring there's so much and it's all so good why bother but back in the ancient times which is what my son calls the sixties when I bring them up though I confess I talk about those times a lot but they were good gentle times but thoughtless was when I learned to value hemp and share it and savor it."

Dunford exhaled, feeling nothing yet. He coughed, then again. "I'll check your *spaogetto*." He returned the cannabis to her, then stood up and went to the stove, hearing the pasta sizzling above the flame. French fried spaghetti. He snorted.

"Just mix yours back in the pot," she suggested.

"But I seasoned mine and put cheese on it." Sound whiney. Good idea, but don't.

"Whatever you do, Dunford, I can live with. You got a good draw this time. It tastes of the earth. I already hear the hum."

"The hum?" he asked from the stove.

"The cosmic hum. Whenever I smoke hemp, if it's in a peaceful place with peaceful people, I can hear the cosmos humming."

"What's it humming?" Peaceful? Me?

"How do you know she's an it?"

Her words entered his ear, but did not stick; he had become engrossed in the pasta, warming the browned bits of garlic without scorching them, stirring the spaghetti with a wooden fork, evenly blending the brown bits throughout the coils, wondering if she would enjoy it. He turned off the stove. "Who?"

"Who what?" she asked back, exhaling, filling the air above the kitchen table with soft gray smoke. "I better light an incense. Ever notice how funky hemp smells when you come into a room and catch a whiff? But if you're in the room smoking, you can't smell a thing." She dove into her bag again, emerging with a packet of incense. "I can offer you cocomango or pachouli."

"Let's try pachouli." His dry mouth told him that the cannabis had started to work on him. He turned back to the stove and served her plate, brought it and set it before her.

She lit a stick of incense with her lighter, saw it catch, shook out the flame, sweet pungent smoke billowing. She passed him the cannabis. "You can finish it. This looks good. I try not to eat after six, but I'll skip breakfast tomorrow."

Dunford stared at the halfinch stub clamped between his thumb and index finger, the ember fading. He puffed it awake, and then inhaled smoke, which this time did not catch in his throat. He held his breath, feeling his heart pounding louder, sending the smoke throughout his body in tiny gray tubes. Getting high like a mothermugger after all these years! Wow.

Renka Bravo had begun to eat, adroitly wrapping pasta

round her fork as she deliberately chewed what she already had in her mouth, eyes smiling at him. He exhaled, dropped the stub in the ashtray. "I forget how many classes you taught." Maybe she'll tell me what.

She swallowed. "Three classes of fifteen. Nice bunch."

"I guess I like mine too." He looked at his cold plate, nudged it with his fork, found it stiff.

"You really should've put it back into the pot." She had followed his eyes, surmising his thoughts.

"It's no big deal. I had enough before you came. D'you want some salad?"

"In Europe, sir, they serve the salad, then the pasta." She paused, looked stricken. "I'm sorry. That was just nervous chatter."

"Why're you nervous?" Dunford put down his fork. Disarmed.

"I usually just let the words spill out, but now I don't know where to begin at the beginning I've seen you around campus many times and I think once we even had a chat at a faculty tea sharing a joke about Professor Winograd's hairiness I think his name is and you and I stood there and cracked up so from then on I hoped we'd end up at the same place sometime and get properly introduced and become friends though in two years that never happened til I bumped into you at the supermarket tonight I just said to myself, Renka, now or never and responded to your comment and called to ask you to the open house when what I really want is to ask you out on a date."

"On a date? Times sure change. I don't think anybody ever asked me out on a date before." The idea genuinely amused him. "I never did quite ask some out, but we found ourselves going out. Here I am fifty years old and getting asked out for the first time."

"You're making fun of me." She frowned playfully. "Well, just reward me for asking. Say yes."

"Shouldn't I find out what kind of date you have in mind before I answer. Don't women usually do that?" She laughed; he continued: "I always wondered what it would feel like to sit there and be asked. Pardon me if I wax professorial about this, but the first terror a teenaged boy knows, at least in my generation, is the terror of asking out a girl. These kids aren't like that anymore. I observe the girls routinely asking boys out on dates. But in my time? Which must be before your time." She looked about forty. Ten when she. Atom (1945!) Bomb Summer. "In those ancient times, round 1950, a girl never asked out a boy. Including bad girls."

"You consider me bad for asking?"

"Not at all. If anything, brave. Risking rejection." Dunford sipped his cranberry juice, realizing how many years had gone by since he's had a guardsdown kitchen conversation with a woman, his mother, his sister, once with Wendy Whitman, a few times with Harriet Lewis. "And I feel relieved not to have to ask. I noticed you in the supermarket, holding a bunch of grapes, and I think I talked to you first, but I never would've asked you out. Not then and there. You might scream or something."

"That's an exaggeration, don't you think?"

"A strange . . . man making advances to you? You know."

She narrowed her eyes, a camera focusing sharp, trying to see his meaning. "You don't mean the race thing, do you?"

"Well, I grew up in segregated times, even though integrated. Where'd you grow up?"

"Maine."

"Maine?"

She nodded. "My dad snuck me into the Ali-Liston fight."

"You're pretty weird, Renka." He made himself use her name, dared himself the intimacy of it. "Almost as weird as me, except you don't seem to try to hide it."

"Does that mean you'll go out with me?"

"You're right. Boys are like that. Never take No for an answer. I always gave up at the first No."

"Take it from me, Dunford, we only go out with that kind because we get tired of fighting them off. And the nice guys like you don't ask. You tired yet?"

Like a cold draft of wind seeping in, Dunford sensed suspicion within himself, startling him: What did this woman really want? "You mean like go to the movies or something? You know that if we go to a movie, somebody on campus will start whispering about our dating. We'll immediately get invited to everything as a couple, a mixed couple at that."

"A mixed couple of what?" she mocked softly. "Nuts?"

"Maybe it'll just be better for me to come to the open house with my niece and you know, leave it at that."

Abruptly she got up. "I'll settle for that, Dunford. And make sure you do bring your niece. This'll be about the only intercultural thing to happen around her for the next three months. Everybody who's coming from somewhere else ends up at International House." She took up her rustcolored coat and draped it round her shoulders, then wriggled her arms into the sleeves, her sparkling fingers out at the cuffs. "And she's definitely from somewhere else."

Stunned by the suddenness of her leavingtaking, Dunford remained seated. "I will. When is it again?"

"Christmas afternoon around three. You know how to get to International House, don't you? It's across from Winooski High School. That's another reason why your niece would want to come. She'll probably end up at Winooski. My son's a freshman there. They seem to tolerate diversity."

"Did I tell you my niece is staying?"

"Didn't you?"

"I don't think so, but as matter of fact she's staying til June."

"She'll have a good time." She adjusted her coat on her shoulders, buttoned the top two buttons, bronze halfdollar sized. "Dunford, I thank you for the *spaogetto* and your hospitality." She extended her hand.

He wondered if he had said the wrong thing. "Sure. You're welcome." He stood up, took her hand, shook it. "Do you have to leave?"

"Must be around eleven, right? Everybody at home'll wonder what planet I stopped off at. But I'll come back, Dunford, if that prospect interests you."

"Sure." He felt his mouth hanging open, closed it, licked his lips. "I hope I didn't . . ."

"You didn't." She leaned toward him exotic aroma coming close and kissed his cheek softly; he did not shrink. "We covered enough ground for one evening."

Dunford followed as she swept out of the kitchen to the front door, which she halted before and let him open. "I never mess with locks I don't know. You know your locks better than I do."

He decided he liked her, encouraged her. "My locks're easy to unlock when you get to know them."

"Looking forward to it, Dunford." She stepped into the cold. "Goodnight."

Renka Bravo navigated the icy front steps and strode down his salted front walk, kept clean by a neighborhood subteenager whom Dunford paid twenty dollars each snowfall. At her car, an English Drover capable of going from the North Pole to the headwaters of the Amazon on one change of oil, she turned and waved, then opened the door and slid inside. The engine roared without false start. Into the night, away she cruised, leaving Dunford in his doorway, on the threshold between lifefreezing chill and lifegiving warmth, trying to come up with an adjective to describe her. Exotic. Beautiful. Well perhaps not quite beautiful. But pretty falls short. Intelligent? Definitely. Where do adjectives hide when you really need them? Intuitive. She sounds so working-class or maybe that's the Maine accent or even Frenchcanadian. Cajun no after they got to Louisiana they became. Canook. Shapely. Too solid a build for a dancer. Not much shape to see under that coat or caftan. Muumuu? OoooOooo what a little moomoo can do. Moomoo Moonlight in Vermont. Around new moon now or it just went down. Don't solstice and new moon go together? Didn't winter start round sundown? At the airport waiting Merry came Christmas in the cold. Wind whipped. Nearly naked. Wonder how she knew all that stuff about Merry and figs.

He turned into his warm house, grateful. He hated the cold, ended up settling in the cold northeast corner of the Republic, especially when he'd turned down job offers that would've taken him to warmer places. Reaching back, he launched the door toward its jam, heard it click shut.

"Charles! Wait!"

Through the door's diamondshaped window, Dunford spied the speaker, shambling up the walk, bearded face in the shadows of a black parkahood, mounting the front steps, a sneer in the middle of wiry beard, flecks of powdered sugar on his mustache, peering through the glass. "Charles!"

Stifling a sigh, Dunford opened the door. "Hello, Raymond, what brings you out so late?" What a night! Merry. Bravo. Solstice. Saturnalia. All bets off.

Sacrificed the king. Crook.

"Important matters, Charles!" Raymond Winograd exhaled a cloud of soursmelling steam. "The integrity of the department is tied to the stake and the witches are looking for matches." He pushed by Dunford into the house. "Looking for matches, Charles!" Dunford closed the door, but stood near it. Two plates in the kitchen. Did she leave the? On the table? Offer him booze. "D'you want some cognac, Raymond?" Enforced intimacy of address. My boss. S.O.B. spelled backways Redd Foxx said. My boss. No more no less.

Raymond Winograd stopped dead in his tracks.

"Coke?"

"No, but I think I have Dr. Pepson. I said cognac." He remained by the front door. "I see you're really agitated about this situation. Just park yourself in that good leather chair, and I'll pour you some cognac straight from France, and if I can help out . . ."

"Thanks, Charles." Winograd went down the two steps into the livingroom, the torn cover of a new paperback flapping from his pocket, and sat in the leather chair closest to the loaded unlit fireplace.

Dunford followed now and went to his liquor cabinet, trying to remember when he'd started the bottle of cognac. That first really cold day in November, feeling blue, opening it, sipping some, reading the first masterpiece by the youthful Dupukshamin, *The Hermit,* from 1820 round the time he met the love of his life, the delightful Laraonsa Bellao. *Timber! came the far cry . . .*

"Up a little late yourself, Charles," Winograd commented, relaxing into the squeaking leather, unzipping his black parka. "I would've hated to wake you, but this matter couldn't wait til our meeting tomorrow."

Dunford poured a cognac, speaking over his shoulder. "So this meeting takes the place of the one scheduled for tom—"

"Suzu led me to believe you had some reason of your own to drop by the office tomorrow."

"Me?" He handed Winograd the cognac, remembering the messages still unerased on his machine, realizing like lightning from on high that at bottom his b.o.S.S. (and that's two of them) wanted to know how much money he could expect from Dunford toward the cost of his second VCR. Suzu the secretary, who kept the department of CompLit running smoothly despite the chaos that Winograd habitually left in his wash, had voiced no great alarm about any threat to the integrity of the department. Therefore, none existed. "Oh, I guess I did. I had something to give Suzu. I must be tired. My niece arrived today." He sat on an ottoman opposite the chairman.

"Looking for matches, Charles." He sniffed, sipped the amber liquid. "But I won't let them burn down what I've tried to build up these last seven years." He sipped again. "Damn witches can get on their brooms and fly straight to Hell!"

"Which witches do you mean, Raymond?" Dunford felt a yawn coming, the phoney crisis failing to awaken his interest. "Any witches I know?"

Winograd shot him a glance. "You don't seem to take this threat—"

"I don't know what it is, Raymond." His own testiness surprised him. Saturnalia. All bets off.

"They want me to hire a damn gay, Charles! A mincing fag or one of those bulldaggers."

"Who does?"

"Sparks, Pointer, and Lifski. Bad enough they have the twentieth century locked up. Now they want a gay studies component added. And they have the dean's ear. Frankly," he lowered his voice, a sure sign he intended to lie, "I'd wanted to bring in a black and a caribbean man, Sir Fitzroy Wyndham." He stared at Dunford, expecting some reaction. "You know

Wyndham's work on Kay McClaude and the Harlem Renaissance of course."

"Of course." Dry stuff, Dunford had decided. Five hundred pages to say what he could've said in fifty. Footnotes to beat the band. The immigrant thing but in racial terms. "Some interesting insights."

"Well, Charles, do I have your support?" Winograd sipped again, Dunford noticing anew the powder on his mustache. "I know the dean likes you."

"Whom do Sparks, Pointer and Lifski want you to hire?" Actually he held these particular witches in high regard. They seemed genuinely to keep their students' welfare in mind. He'd found their scholarship impeccable, notably Lifski, who often came up with valid, if unorthodox ways to compare the literature of one culture to another.

"They just want to make it seem as if my administration isn't comprehensive. As if we had a bias." Winograd drained his goblet. "They just want to stick it to me, like I'm some sort of chauvinist. Frankly, I think Lifski has the hots for me, and provokes the others."

"It always comes back to sex, doesn't it, Raymond." He watched the chairman finishing the cognac, enjoying the unstressful distance the cannabis gave him from the other. Only wants his kickback. How much to give? Can manage twenty. "So you have a lot of room, Raymond. It's not as if they have somebody dangerous like Jane Grotonson in mind." Extortionist.

"At least not yet." He stared at his empty glass goblet. "Sir Fitzroy Wyndham's got a wife and children, but maybe he's a fag too."

"They outfoxed themselves, Raymond. They didn't have a specific candidate ready, so you still make the final decision.

You have the chance to find someone you can work with smoothly." Pay off one of his chums. Spin him into it and he'll think he stepped boldly forward. "Perhaps you really can find someone who's gay and Black."

"And a goddamn woman!" The chairman laughed coarsely. "I'll give them a gay black female! Maybe crippled. Four birds with one stone!"

"That's the ticket, Raymond, make the best of the situation."

Winograd shut off his boisterous laughter. "Yes." His eyes narrowed. "But how do you come to see it that way, Charles? Where do your true allegiances rest?" He sniffed, reached out his goblet for a refill.

Dunford took the goblet and got up quickly, thankful for the time to form his answer to the question, which had taken him by surprise. "My true allegiances?"

"Yes. Perhaps I shouldn't say this, but then, why not? I hold with Socrates: To thine ownself be true."

"But that was Shake—" Dunford mumbled, pouring cognac.

"I try to make myself happy, Charles. But that doesn't mean I shortchange others. I do my best for myself and the department. When I insist that the department needs the best VCR that money can buy, I don't just have my own needs in mind. Everybody in the department will get use out of it. It's portable."

"Did anyone really question that, Raymond?" Dunford returned to his ottoman, handed Winograd his cognac, then sat. "Of course what's good for you is goo—"

"Those damn witches! You can trace all the rumors back to their coven." He sipped. "But what about your allegiances, Charles?"

"Mine? I guess I have many." In reality none that jumped to mind. Know he means race. Prefer to call it culture, but that's too abstract for him. The college, the department? Too glib. The kids? Like 'em but. Don't live at home, New York. Convent Ave. Mom. Dad dead. Peter. Connie. The boys. Merry. "But I guess I'd have to say my family."

"Admirable," Winograd commented, disappointment evident in his intonation. "Truly admirable, but I didn't mean quite so profound."

"I know what side my toast is buttered on." Dunford winked. My boss no more no less. Fraud. Crook.

"Toast!" He enjoyed the racial twist. "Well said, Charles. Love the reference to your darker complexion."

"Thanks, Raymond."

"Glad to know I can count on your support." He relaxed into the leather, swirling his cognac. "You can't make it in this world without staunch allies. I value your support. I value it doubly because when they brought me in as chairman, I know that were it not for the, shall we say, exclusive advancement policies of the college, you might've secured the position for yourself. After all, you filled in after my predecessor dropped dead. You knew the job. Even so, I never for a minute felt you trying to undermine me. You just pitched right in."

"I knew they wouldn't appoint me." Dunford shrugged, monitoring any bitterness that might come into his voice, found none, no surprise. "Actually, I didn't mind the honor or the money, but I didn't want the hassle. It takes—"

"But didn't you harbor some hopes?"

"Believe me, Raymond, I didn't." He wondered why he wanted to reassure Winograd when something urged him to make the other man squirm. But what the heck. Getting tired now. Winding down. Plus, filling in for fallen professor Phillips, he had quickly realized that the job involved long hours of chitchat and miles of paperwork, even with the dependable Suzu taking care of the day-to-day. A teacher might have to grade students, but a department chairman had to grade teachers, making decisions (he had seen in at least two cases) which had driven people to suicide. "Scholarship's my strength, Raymond, not administration."

"Well, I'm no slouch as a scholar myself, Charles."

"Of course, Raymond, why just this evening I saw you in the Yankee Bear Bookstore, picking up two books."

"Picking up two books?"

"Standing by the front door. You had them in your hand." Dunford paused, inserting the ice pick slowly. "Then . . . the light changed. In fact, I noticed you've torn your cover. Of your book."

Winograd straightened his spine and looked down over his beard at his bulging parka pocket, stuffed the protruding cover back into the black hole. "Damn books don't hold up," he muttered. "Rip the day you . . . buy them."

Dunford stood up, realizing he had already learned something from Renka Bravo. "Before I forget, let me get that envelope for Suzu. Excuse me a minute." He took the two steps at a bound and made a left through the swinging doors into the kitchen. Film canister next to the salt and pepper. Good thing to steer him into. Might've. He scooped it up and into his pocket, feeling the cannabis shifting around inside, like beans inside a maraca. Quickly he took the oily plates to the sink. Dump that later. Or put it back for tomorrow. In a minute.

On his knickknack shelves, he found a clean envelope and into it deposited his last twenty-dollar bill, resolving to visit Capitol Savings and Loan (open from nine til noon on Monday) in the morning while giving Merry a sunlit tour of the town. Have a heart to heart about. Just some quick remarks. He wrote a brief note: Suzu, enclosed please find something toward our esteemed chairman's seventh-anniversary present. Regards, C. Dunford—then folding and putting the note into the envelope next to the bill, licking and sealing it, addressing it simply: Suzu.

Dunford hurried back into the foyer, found Winograd reclining in the leather chair, his eyes halfclosed, his snifter cupped loosely in his hand, stem and base down through his fingers.

"Here it is, Raymond." He extended the envelope, but did not come down the steps into the livingroom, wanting Winograd gotten up and gone. "Raymond? You asleep?"

The chairman shook his head, sitting up and zipping his black parka. "Really got off there, Charles. Loads on my mind."

"Enough to bring you outside late on a cold night." Dunford stood his ground. Want him on his feet now. Acting strange. Out into the cold night. Gone. "You too tired to drive, Raymond? Want me to call you a taxi?"

"Not necessary." The chairman struggled to his feet as if lifting a heavy weight. "What I really need is a vacation. In the sun. Away from Lilith."

"On second thought, I don't really have to trouble you with this." Dunford let his hand fall to his thigh, turned toward the front door, hoping the scent of money would encourage Winograd to follow him "I can just as well take this—"

"Save yourself the trip, Charles." Dunford heard footsteps behind him, crossing from carpet to wood, climbing two steps. "You said you didn't have to stop by the office except for this." Dunford turned and handed the envelope to Chairman Winograd. Last twenty. And took two books too. Crook.

The chairman tested the envelope's thickness with his fingers. "Not writing Suzu any mash notes, are you Charles? You know how we feel about intradepartmental romance."

Dunford smiled, forcing himself to take Winograd's gibe goodnaturedly. "I didn't know the department had a policy on intradepartmental romance. Isn't Lilith still subbing—"

"Only joking, Charles." He laughed, raising the envelope to his face. "Just felt a little thick. This about department business?"

Dunford wondered what Winograd wanted to hear, decided only the money mattered. "Actually it's my last twenty dollars, going toward a Christmas gift for a colleague." Christmas gift should make him wonder. Tear into it anyway, lie about it later. Just the money wrapped in a note. Envelope torn when Charles gave it to me. Next week ask Suzu how. Dunford opened the front door to the longest night of winter.

The chairman had stuffed the envelope into his parka pocket along with his stolen books. "Very happy to save you a trip, Charles."

"And many thanks for it, Raymond." Wind gusted in, swirling round Dunford's ankles. "One less stop tomorrow."

"Well, you have a merry Christmas, Charles."

"And you too. Goodnight, Raymond."

"Goodnight, Charles." The chairman stepped over the threshold, ducked his shoulder as if to turn back for yet another final word, but Dunford closed the door quickly, snapped off the foyer light and peered through the diamondshaped window at the hunched and hooded figure disappearing into the darkness. In a moment, he heard the motor of his vehicle, an old man agonizingly clearing his throat, then the gears wheezily engaging, grumbling away.

Dunford retrieved Winograd's snifter, gave his livingroom a check, then returned to the kitchen, fifteen minutes' cleaning ahead of him. He covered the salad with clinging plastic and put it into the fridge, hoping it would keep for seventeen hours but experience reminding him that it wouldn't. Lettuce gets dark and tomatoes go mushy. Anyway try. Too much stuff in here. In Smepriroa never had more than a tin or two some bread. Oil. Now just look. Eat vegetables til Christmas afternoon Monday Tuesday Wednesday afternoon. Let Merry eat what she wants. Knows herself. Know she like figs. Funny grainy chewy fruit. Gnarled little bush. Bravo brilliant about figs. Forgot to tell her.

He pondered the remaining coils of spaghetti, in the pot, in his bowl. Somehow Renka Bravo had found the time to finish hers. Exotic imperfectly beautiful woman. Hazel eyes. Steady on her feet like she'd walked some miles in Maine probably not a dancer looking like a duck waddling. More Reupeon peasant in sandals like Merry in this freezing cold. Does cannabis warm the body?

Sweating in cold weather. Just ask her how often. Just a few words. Tell her to take care.

Dunford decided to dispose of his cold bowl of spaghetti, but save the spaghetti in the pot, putting it into a small covered container in the fridge. Will dry but tomorrow steam will. Run water nice and hot. Suds cut the oil. At the sink he squeezed out some dish detergent and filled his little tub with bubbles. He stacked the plates, bunched the silverware and, remembering Mrs. Dale in seventh-grade cooking; plunged first the glass, the coffee mug and the snifter into soapy water. Ouch. Hot. But not too. Just fish out the rag and let it cool enough to wipe these lip prints one mine one Renka Bravo one his. No lipstick. Wonder if lip prints as distinctive as fingerprints as distinctive as voice prints as distinctive as. Everything. Not the same as anything else. All different. He washed the vessels, then rinsed and set them draining upside down in the yellow drainbasket.

Next the silverware, after the cups and glasses. First lesson, washing utensils: glasses-silver-plates-pots, from cleanest to greasiest, making the soap last, Mrs. Dale in pincenez and brown hair curled in a bun like a danish behind her left ear but never the nape of her neck old lady style. Nice hips no tits.

Mrs. Dale trying to keep her zing, but out of place at Shaddy Bend School. Wore too much makeup. And the pincenez. Haunted the basement cooking room for years. Foto in old yearbooks. No sign of Mr. Dale. No Dale over hill and down. Maybe dead. We wondered what they did in bed.

His hands tingling in the incubating suds swabbing the spaghetti bowls, he remembered when he and his school friends, white kids from Westchester and Central Park West, talked only of sports and sex, allamerican boys, fifth grade: Mrs. Yule. All drooled to get into bed with Mrs. Yule. Well not drooled. But if you really had to have sex, Mrs. Yule might make the first experience palatable, even pleasurable. Boys only marching to the Science Room on the third floor so Mrs. Yule could tell us about sex. Who told the girls? Had boners bathing and waking up but didn't know what you really did with one. Just felt good. Now Mrs. Yule's shapely legs crossed nervous herself probably knowing our young minds explaining what you could do with a boner. Same as the cats on 148th street did yowling sliding that boner in and out of shapely blondehaired blueyed Mrs. Yule's shapely body while she coached you through it. Sitting spellbound getting a boner right there in the Science Room. Can't remember one word except Sex itself but all the words kindling the feelings. Come to me, little Chig, let me show you how. Now. Wow. That first time really with Bubbles. Better than the first kiss with Shirley first love. Better than many feel-ups with Avis naked in the bed careful not to come when her parents went away. Better. Better. Bubbles.

"Beatrice Bubbles Bailey. Went to California," Dunford sighed aloud as he ran steelwool inside the bottom of the pot where he'd combined garlic and spaghetti, getting up bits of pasta. The black skillet he wiped with two pages from the *Burlington Bugle,* then the wrungout dishrag. "Bubbles Bailey. What an armful!"

What a body! he thought. How she felt! Want to say like a sponge but much firmer like a real sponge from the sea bottom more solid than airy. Organic. And madly wiggling and wickedly moaning. Orgasmic too: seemed sincerely to love to. Exhausting. Funny. Met at that party round the corner from home on Riverside and attached herself to me. Can't remember who intro'd us. Somehow found myself compelled to take her home. Had her own place on 150th near Amsterdam. Top floor. Loved to screw. Said so. Proud of it.

"What a body!" he exclaimed. Spoiled me. Thought all woman like that. Open. Enjoying to give it up but not slutty. These days they'd call Bubbles a sex addict. But never thought she gave it up to just anybody. Never caught anything from her. California, here come Bubbles. Had some guy out there waiting. Only in New York to get a degree. Went to join him.

Dunford smiled, bemused, memories of his passionate two-month affair with Beatrice Bailey warming his blood, with damp dishrag wiping his surfaces, stovetop, sink drain, vinyl counter below wooden cabinets. "Twenty that summer of fiftyfive. She must've been about twentyfive," he said to the wall above the kitchen sink where he had already tacked his new 1986 Aubuchon Hardware store calendar. "Thirty years ago and only a dozen since Bubbles." He shook his head, surveyed his kitchen, decided it would pass Mrs. Dale's inspection, then crossed to the door and exiting reached back and snapped off the rosetinted light.

In the foyer at the foot of the stairs he paused under amber now and listened to his house around him and the quiet night beyond. Bubbles didn't keep him a secret his picture right by the bed we. Wonder if she kept me a secret? Don't go falling in love with me or anything dumb like that, little boy. Not no boy no more. Didn't tell her but she guessed. Let me do it again right away like learning to ride a bike. Didn't know what to do, huh? Don't worry bout a thing. Next train due in about thirty minutes. All aboard. Boner ached that summer. While Avis went to Arawaka. Going steady since high school. Sophomores.

Dunford ascended the stairs to the second floor, wood creaking underfoot, annoying years before but now acknowledged as a trusted sound of the house. Never told Avis. We wanted to do it with each other first. Came close a couple times but never put it inside just felt her all over kissed her everywhere loved her. Avis in the sun like caramel little breasts great legs five-two one-ten. Loved her. Returned from Arawaka toffeecolored with a cute little accent. So how do you, eeee? Smelled like curry. Really loved her. Always loved her. Never told her about Bubbles. Too jealous though when she did the same would justify her way out of it. Like almost with that guy in her class one night after chorus or something he gave her a lift and they stopped to look at the Hudson or some shit like that. Got his hand in her panties. Would get into tight spots. Have to do things. Loved her no matter. When she got away to Poughkeepsie we started. Way up high in that tall dorm. Couldn't wait both loved it and me knowing what to do. Avis. Had muscle. But a bit of a bitch. Spoiled and oppressed at the same time. Bound. Had everything planned whole life wound tight on a spool. All planned out til twothousandten, winters in Ardsley, summers in Sag Harbor two kids in private school like us again. Did it too without me. Married twice one white one brown. Saw her that last trip to New York. Crazy about tennis. Trim as ever. Hard as nails.

Entering his bedroom Dunford turned on the light, a lamp on his bedtable, then chest to dresser, inspected the strewn contents of his pantspockets, emptied on the evening's first trip to the second floor: his keys, car, campus office, post office box, house, on a ring. Give Merry the extra to the front door. Might want to roam. Likes cold might like a solo walk in snow. Got to trust her. Stay in much as possible myself. Wonder where she gets that from Clive roots in Arawaka. But he spent time in Canada colder than here. Connie likes to stay warm and cozy. We both stayed in all winter when she came to Smepriroa to have Bigbro. Nice of Clive to adopt him later but turns out we need a male Dunford.

Unless Peter. But what does brother Peter say? Revolutionaries should never take wives. Or me why didn't I ever? Getting married having kids.

Dunford saw himself as a father, in a hammock on his front porch in summer, relaxing and rocking, and in the yard—greener grass than he'd ever actually cultivated—his kids, boy of course to continue the name, and a girl, and another girl yes two girls. Three's enough ten and eight and six. Boy in the middle different from Connie and Peter and me. New start. But he never imagined a wife after Avis. Getting married and having kids didn't seem viable after Avis. Like part of the breakup involved leaving the idea of marriage in her care. Couldn't see it any other way. Her way or no way.

Dunford counted his cash, a twenty plus a ten plus seven singles and seventythree cents, two quarters plus two dimes and three dirtsmeared pennies. He reclipped the bills and set them atop the sprawled change. Tolls and parking, ten bucks. Fifteen fortyfive for groceries Write it down tomorrow. Behind in moneybook a few days. Better have Papaleo look at that right rear tyre.

Don't forget that house payment in the Christmas madness with basically everything going smooth and they just waiting to pounce and gobble up this landmark and put me out on the street. Funny how Avis made me think of money. Fearfully.

Thirtyseven seventythree. Came down to cash though. How you make it and how you spend it we never agreed. Avis always went for mahogany.

Dunford much preferred pine. Sitting down on the side of his bed, he undid his belt and the flybuttons of his blue corduroys, pulled his seat out of them and slid his trousers down his legs, over his stockinged feet, staring off into his past as Avis ran away weeping at the news that they would never marry. Avis had olympic-level runners in her family, men who'd run for the West Indies in the thirties and forties and she ran in her doeskin slippers with the quick steps of a hurdler. With the grace of a deer striding bounding. Didn't want to hurt her but it couldn't work. Didn't feel the same about money. Dunford stood up and wrestled his royal blue lightwool turtleneck sweater over his head, leaving him in white tee shirt and blue boxers and white tube socks with blue stripes. He liked blue and found white underwear easier to keep clean. "But I didn't turn out too bad. Nice house and all. Maybe I didn't become an architect but at least I avoided going to law school," he remarked to the selfimage on the closet door. "At least I saved myself from that."

Chubby Charles. Accursed sagging tits. Shaped like a pear narrow shoulders and fortyfour-inch waist. Tub of guts. Legs like Mr. Walnut. Scrawny arms.

Forearms not so bad but so what. Blubber and wrinkles. Fifty years. Old. Well, young old.

In mashedheel moccasins, Dunford quickstepped down the hall to the bathroom, the urge to urinate gathering itself in his loins. Urge. Urge Dr. Dalph called that feeling though usually lots of piss comes pouring out of me. Haven't pissed since four. Too long. Remember to drink water these days don't forget in the Christmas madness two cups right away in the morning. Close the door. Lady's present. Top and seat up and get him out and let him rip. "Ah!" Dunford sighed above the drizzle of clear urine flowing from him into the toilet bowl. Okay. Clear as spring water. Not pink. Not yellow. No mucous. No clots. Clear. Thank you, God. Dunford twisted on the hot water, waited til it turned from cold to tepid, then drank a cup in eight swallows.

He unwrapped and wet his toothbrush then squeezed some toothpaste onto the bristles. Didn't leave Avis for another girl so didn't screw anyone for a long. Peter would've feathered a new nest first but not me. Even going to Reupeo. Principled jerk! Walking around Reupeo with blue balls for almost a year. Chig the travelling celibate. The old days. Not all like Bubbles especially in Reupeo. You had to have something to offer. Hard to get a girl to do it unless you practically proposed. Or had money. Fiftyseven. Had to say you loved her even if she knew you lied. Or had money. He worked methodically on his teeth, insidebottom insidetop outsidetop outsidebottom, then again, then again, then spitting and rinsing and spitting, then did an inspection for smoothness and bits of garlic in the crevices with the tip of his tongue. He drank a second cup of water.

Next he filled the basin with warm water and immersed his washrag. Wonder if Sophia ever told Dr. Goldtree we had probably not. No reason to. Just think I didn't get laid that year at all after Avis until I got those cavities. Never met anybody who wanted. Felt bad about Avis. Still loved her but didn't like her. Couldn't see anybody seeing me. Got real fat the first time eating my troubles away. Just get fat and troubles remain. Enough is enough and too much spoils. Came back from Reupeo fat and with cavities. Different food. Different water. Different fat toothbrushes. Felt like a broom in your mouth. Had to take my mouth to old Dr. Goldtree Central Park West. Ground floor subway rumbling under. Goldtree slightly too crass for the Shaddy Bend crowd but making big money with movie stars flying in from California to let doctor Goldtree give their teeth the Goldtree Smile. Doing mine since fourth grade. Mrs. Goldtree and Mom always got along sitting together at Shaddy Bend Parents Society meetings. Mrs. Goldtree grown up on the Concourse near the Stadium. Twinkle in her eye. Smoked like a furnace. Voice like a tyre iron. Tell your mother to call me, darling. I'm in the book under Esther Goldtree. Say hi to your dad too. Always had some reason to come to school this committee or that. She ran the real estate end while the doc did teeth. Read they gave a million to Israel. Nothing now. But in nineteensixty? Sophia wore nothing but cashmere sweaters in the winter. Nice tits in cashmere. Never thought she saw me later said she did.

We all thought she started screwing Garth Worthheim in sixth form but she said not. Like Avis and me heavypetting and naked and feeling up each other. Garth always came to school Mondays looking smug like he'd screwed her over the weekend. She said she'd jerked him off but didn't screw anybody til freshman year at Brandeis. A Harvard guy w. a. s. p. preppy slumming. Had a name like Coolidge or Taylor, Jackson, or Johnson a president's name. Thought he'd marry her. Same old story. Weekend she thought he'd take her home to meet the family in Newport he broke it off and still wanted to screw her after he told her. Breaking the heart of a Jewish princess gave him a little pink boner. Swell guy. Reg fell. Preppy swine.

A last time he wrung his washrag and wiped his face, looking into his own brown eyes, whites offwhite. Tired too much reading kilometers of empty pages. But what did that one kid write? *Ulysses* is the kind of a book I wouldn't read if I didn't have to because it takes too long for nothing to happen. Yes. Yes. Ignorantly brilliant. But rare.

Sniffing at his armpits, Dunford considered taking a bath but decided he'd got only moderately odorous in a day of reading and driving and shopping and cooking. He could sleep with the scent of his encounters and take a shower in the morning, perhaps after doing some light stretching exercises he'd read about recently. Work your way up from your ankles studies showing the old don't get weak they get stiff. When did you last touch your toes or even see them? Meet any steps lately you couldn't climb? Tennis any fun? Or do you hang on the net gasping for air ensnared in fatigue? Stretching exercises adapted from hatha yoga. Come to think Sophia did yoga.

Dunford returned to his room, sat, and removed his socks. Sleep in the rest. Start fresh in the morning. Nice and warm anyway against cold sheets. Could look in on her see if she stayed covered but window closed. Enough for today. Strange the way cannabis came back into my life after ten years. When did I first?

"Sophia Goldtree turned me on!" Dunford realized aloud. "That same day!" September fiftyeight just back bringing home Connie and Bigbro. Connie met Clive that next New Year's Eve. Got married in June. Clive Junior in sixtytwo. Then Merry came in sixtyeight. Birthday coming up might give her a party. Visited them quiet watchful baby in a playpen never cried placid or cheerful. Likeable little kid. Still. Sipping wine and smoking cannabis on Clive and Connie's back porch ten years after Sophia turned me on first time. Going to the dentist never thinking you'll end up getting high and laid all in one day filling all kinds of cavities. Sophia subbing for Dr. Goldtree's nurse on her lunch hour nice breasts in white silk blouse. First white woman but never thought of her as white. Just Sophia who I grew up with since first grade flat chest then. O Chig I'm so thrilled to see you again I'll wait for you and we'll have lunch. How could I say no? To Sophia Goldtree who went to school with me for twelve straight years? Whose dad filled holes in my teeth since 1945. Went to lunch old Chinese restaurant on Broadway in the seventies. Later like Beatniks buying chianti and a corkscrew and going to Riverside Park her idea. Sitting talking all afternoon getting smashed. Come on home for dinner high above Central Park shadows reaching out across the redflecked green treetops. Red sun in glass windows on Fifth and beyond. Pulled out a fistful of yellow cannabis just back from Acapulco. Gold grass. What about your parents? Gone to the Catskills for the weekend. Won't get back til Monday night.

"What a weekend!" Cut gold grass with sharp kitchen knife on wood cutting board like chopping parsley for garnish and then rolled two dozen thin smokes as even and equal as a machine like coming out of a box Sophia had a gift for it. Fell into a soft chair in front of the reservoir like a silver tray and flamingo flaming windows and lit two smokes and passed me one. Afraid. Heard about it saw it once in college three times in Reupeo the first trip. Never felt the situation the people trustworthy. Trusted Sophia if anything happened wouldn't just drift away and leave me to die alone and had perfect conical silkcovered breasts and perfect scores on two of her SATs and lived a quartermile above the nearest policeman in a building with an Irish doorman—took that first cannabis. Quickly got blasted and silly playful cares turning trivial laughable. Knew now I'd do okay in grad school just plug away like always go to classes and get your papers in on time no big deal. Forgot about Avis. Forgot about Pop. Still didn't know what Sophia had in mind.

Found out quick. Content to try cannabis in a safe place and eat some cheese and crackers and drink some more wine and then stagger home. "What a weekend!"

Outside the window through black trees and across the valley, Dunford saw the nightlit golden dome of the State Capitol, a bonewhite breast in a golden bra's cup thrust into the eye of the black newmoon starchilled heavens. A white figure stood atop the dome he knew but perceived it only as a jagged vertical ornament and did not know what god or human stood there represented. Near trees took up most of his window and gave only a peephole to view, like looking into a nighttime Easter egg scene. He reached out and snapped off the bedtable lamp, gazed at the faraway sleeping government a moment longer, sighed, then allowed his body to fall back onto bed, bouncing, to rest.

Just lie here a minute outside the covers house not cold cooling. Refreshing like floating on my back fat good for that. Should use the college pool more but coming out into the cold with wet hair. Catch cold. Sophia's soft cool body underneath me like all flesh no bones. Different than Avis or Bubbles. No muscle. Sucked my boner like a lollypop. Grunted and moaned like a stuck piglet from deep inside as me plunging into her. Wow. What a weekend. Finally went out Monday afternoon walked in the park before her parents. After that Sophia came to my place on hundredninth walking distance to Kings College. Smoking and screwing brought out the lust in me with her. Could've married Bubbles but. Almost married Avis. Too late with Sophia perfect breasts and all.

Loved to screw her docking inside her. Never ever said we went steady just steady screwing once twice a week a relief. For her too said so. Went to a few movies sometimes a play. Didn't like feeling people staring at us mixed couple now and then once a scraggly stranger lurching out of a doorway to scold her for going out with a nigger. Sophia suddenly snarling, Go fuck Mengele, you nazi bitch! Woman that time me standing there like a lump. Never knew what to feel. Anger seemed silly.

Person so obviously stupid shabby. Laughable. Like the COLORED sign. Yet people died. The stupid shabby scraggly face of racism a fancy name for ignorance on the hoof. Nowadays people like that carry guns blow you away because you don't wear a necktie. Or do. Or whatever. Or. Roar raw oar ore awe or roar.

The old hermit better crawl under the covers now feeling the house of the cold getting to me. The house of the cold? Drifting off cold and catch a cold. Sophia just turned cold one week grunting and cooing and the next week we aren't going anywhere after three years but we're cozy where we are. Are we? Now I find I look in two eyes of a stranger don't know her anymore. This isn't working for me anymore. What happened between the lust time and this? Not just talking about sex going nowhere. But nowhere's somewhere if you're there. Witty but no matter mind made up no compromise contemplated cunt counter closed bye bye blackbird be be bitch. O well.

Life turned topsyturvy had a routine going now gone steady life steady work then left a hole. Didn't know how deep I couldn't call it love just cozy for me anyway. Not as bad as she made it seem we had fun. But for her nowhere nothing happening unhappy. Cold. Over like that. Nothing nowhere but absence left a void couldn't avoid it. Nowhere was somewhere. Nothing: Something. Just two friends screwing really liked her enough for me but not for Sophia sew fire so.

So returned to Reupeo and stayed five years sixtyone sixtytwo sixtythree sixtyfour the Assasination sixtyfive. Smepriroa Rome Paris Barcelona Smepriroa discovering Dupukshamin well not discovering really Reupeons revered him called him Old Black didn't hold it against him. Our prince of african kings proud of it made him special. Except easy now no africaos there now rigid customs keep most out and send them home quickquick when they finish whatever just sweep through the quarter round Lao Colaonbein and round up africaos and ship them to one's origins or roar oar awe or some say slavery deep dark dens in remotest parts of Saudafriguay or Sodindianaaahrr.

Rollover on tummy. Lydia. Wendy. Harriet. Lydia like so fire. Wendy a whisp purr. Harriet as Avis was again others was similar. Lydia's copper hair and proper accent. Chaalz she said.

Wendy's dead straight long and black should've given her away no white woman ever had hair like that except Siobhan Maugham and maybe like Wendy she wasn't wonder what would've happened if eye saw all along she was black? But couldn't call her black if we all thought she was white? Brown Harriet like Avis wanted more than I could give surrender all work no fun didn't like to travel vomited strange food needed special soap picky as me about wrong things. Very bright good friend just couldn't leave New Yorkshire. Lydia loved travel copper sun in copper hair time we went to the countryside never closer screwing on blanket under grape arbors rocky soil and knew it she started talking bout Britain even as she slipping on her panties after reaching her limit crossing the channel to Reupeo to sow her wild oats sowed'em so went home. Never for a moment saw it as anything but an excursion to the continent knowing we could only exist in Reupeo. Screwed Wendy only once then she disappeared then reappeared then disappeared never heard of her again searched for her even after meeting Harriet on the slow boat home. Harriet a little nervous but understood after I told her the story. Good years on and off and on and off.

Retreat to Smepriroa again. Five years. Laraonsa named after Dupukshamin's Laraonsa Bellao. Friend lasted four.

Could a brought a back with but wood a pined and died outside Reupeo. Simple peasant girl in big city to study nursing wood a pined across the sea.

Got the job here just six since Vermont ten years thirteen in thirty. Aretha sweet as honey but too churchy. Natalie world's most beautiful eyes but too many problems for me old man. Couldn't flatout handle Chaka's wildwoman act but man could she cook. Tried class with Anita but after few months just looked stagey. Joan delicate as orchid wearing purple haze and gold rings in her ears but had to get out of Vermont or freezedry. And the luscious unattainable Kim a mouth to start the Trojans warring. All so brief. None longer than six months mostly they broke it off not my way by myself with a bomb but a *Timber! came the far cry . . .*

As time goes by beginning to see the light too late now love and marriage go together but not for me alone again naturally going the fool on the hill in my solitude I get along without tea for two by the light of the silvery moonlight in Vermont lost April in Paris the good old summertime September in the rain in autumn in New York in a sentimental mood night and day when they begin the beguine never will I marry.

Give it up give it up give it up lives with wives. No tiny wifeypartnercomradesweety in open apron for meaty chiggy. Neither a perfect successdress exec checkbook running business house land leaving me free to track Alexao Dupukshamin across the vast country of the pages he left for my perusal. *Timber! came the far cry . . .* Neither curvy lippy honey blonde to bear mulatto pikni and spend mula me making from syndicated chatshow. Neither neatbrown husbandette can cook can sew can screw mother of two coffee tan and curly kinky. Neither glidey geisha lotus leaf and absorption into chung-kuo-gai as go-beet-ween. Neither bouncy bronzy board of educated augmenting my thirtyeight with a neat twentyfive kind of like modern my mom with one less mouth because we couldn't quite afford three but okay. Neither newyorkupperwestside wifelife on dental dollars and toasted bagels with grim cheese making maybe one son whiney and mariney named Chaim. Neither peasantleatherboots in small stone hut with brood. Neither none no one. No Zundays at the zoo viziting zebraz and chimpanzeez. No buckslunches at the fastfood cheerilies beaming like cheshires chubby chiggies and chiglettes chomping on chunkychips and chuckchops. No crumbcrushers or stickydigits. No kittens. No kids (not goats) in the house.

O but what about that kid down the hall under Nanny Eva's fierce eye? his soul asked awaking as his body unlaxed and tumbled into slumber. Waiting for a family like me telling tax collector Raymondo about pledging allegiance to family the only thing me coming up with like the hermit in his hovel hearing the far cry thinks himself alone but across the woods hearing the farcrying woodsman comes his future disguised as the pregnant maiden Laraonsa limping in labor to his doorstep and birthing and dying and making him instant father to his own granddaughter though he doesn't know that yet and the reader has to find out how the old hermit once sat on the throne but tried to improve the lot of the serfs angering the nobles who rose up and drove him into exile and his wife betraying him and marrying his brother Roffaolo the Usurper even while carrying the old hermit formerly young king's child and calling it his brother's so even the girl herself never knows it and grows up hating the man she thinks of as her father and finally runs away to the gypsies getting with child but then falling into the lustful clutches of Count Daon who keeps her chained up as his personal slut until he realizes that her gypsy lover has impregnated her and so turns her loose to wander the great forest only the amulet round her neck and the birthmark on her buttock revealing her royal ancestry to the ancient midwife his only friend from the old days and the hermit king him having the same mark and now raising his granddaughter he plotting his return to the throne but weight a minute doesn't this look like the clearing where the old hermit's how's that go? In my head since sunset. Timber! came the far cry of the distant woodsman as the old hermit huddled in his hovel in the darkest corner of the great black Reupeon Forest in the darkest pine grove by the darkest bog in the darkest time . . .

ALSO BY

William Melvin Kelley

DANCERS ON THE SHORE

Dancers on the Shore is the first and only short story collection by William Melvin Kelley and the source from which he drew inspiration for his subsequent novels. Originally published in 1964, this collection includes two linked sets of stories about the Bedlow and Dunford families. They represent the earliest work of William Melvin Kelley and provided a rich source of stories and characters who were to fill out his later novels. Spanning generations from the Deep South during Reconstruction to New York City in the 1960s, these insightful stories depict African American families—their struggles, their heartbreak, and their love.

Fiction

DUNFORDS TRAVELS EVERYWHERES

William Melvin Kelley's final work, this is a Joycean, Rabelaisian romp in which he brings back some of his most memorable characters in a novel of three intertwining stories. Ride on out with Rab and Turt, two o'New Afriquerque's toughfast, ruefast Texnosass Arangers, as they battle Chief Pugmichillo and ricecure Mr. Charcarl Walker-Rider. Cut in on Carlyle Bedlow, wrecker of marriage, saver of souls. Or just chug along with Chig Dunford, product of Harlem and private schools, on the circular voyage of self-discovery that takes him from Europe's Café of One Hand to Harlem's Jack O'Gee's Golden Grouse Bar and Restaurant. Beginning on an August Sunday in one of Europe's strangest cities, *Dunfords Travels Everywheres* but always returns back to the same point—the "Begending"—where Mr. Charcarl's dream becomes Chig Dunford's reality (the "Ivy League Negro" in the world outside the Ivory Tower).

Fiction

DEM

Mitchell Pierce is a well-off New York ad executive whose marriage is falling apart. He no longer feels any passion for his pregnant wife, Tam, and even feels estranged from his toddler son, Jake. Trapped in an unrewarding and loveless life, domestic violence, though not in Mitchell's character, is never very far away, either. Mitchell's life will irrevocably change one day, though, when a young man appears at his apartment door to pick up the family's black maid, Opal, for a date. Cooley, it turns out, is not a stranger to the household. The twins that Tam is carrying are a result of superfecundation—the fertilization of two separate ova by two different males. So when one child is born black and the other white, Mitchell goes on a quest to find Cooley and make him take his baby. In the tradition of Brer Rabbit trickster tales, *dem* enacts a modern-day fable of turning the tables on the white oppressor and inverting the history of miscegenation and subjugation of African Americans.

Fiction

ALSO AVAILABLE

A Different Drummer

A Drop of Patience